A Stench of Poppies

A STENCH OF POPPIES

Ivor Drummond

ST. MARTIN'S PRESS   NEW YORK

Copyright © 1978 by Ivor Drummond
All rights reserved. For information, write:
St. Martin's Press, Inc.,
175 Fifth Ave., New York, N.Y. 10010.
Manufactured in the United States of America

Library of Congress Cataloging in Publication Data

Drummond, Ivor.
    A stench of poppies.

    I.   Title.
PZ4.D7933St   1978   [PR6054.R79]   823'.9'14   77-91888
ISBN 0-312-76147-3

Chapter 1

In the suburbs of Tbilisi (known to the West as Tiflis) stands the Georgian Institute of Agricultural Science: a squat, foursquare building, exceptionally ugly, the most notable monument to Stalinism in that attractive part of Russia between the Black Sea and the Caspian.

Krikor Grotrian, aged in the service of scientific agriculture, walked stiffly along the concrete corridors, which smelled a little of hospital and a little of prison. He was one of the few Armenians in an organization dominated by Georgians; he felt himself to be one of the few real scientists in an organization dominated by bureaucrats. He had been ordered to present himself to the new Director of the Institute, about whom he had heard only that he was a Georgian and a non-scientist. The secretary's voice on the internal telephone had not asked if the time were convenient, if he were in the middle of a tricky experiment or a complex calculation; the arrogant woman had merely required him to report at once to the office of the Director. It was typical. Krikor Grotrian changed his laboratory coat for the jacket of his suit – once a vivid blue and of sharp cut, now shabby, the pockets distended by pens and notebooks – and told his assistant to leave some tea for him.

But the tea would be cold. He waited a long time in the anteroom of the Director's office, under the basilisk eye of the secretary, with other members of the scientific staff likewise summoned. He might have said something to these colleagues, in spite of his resentment of their ethnic hubris; scientist to scientist, they might together have deplored the way they were treated by the bureaucrats; there had been thousands of such conversations, over the years, at café tables and in private apartments; but not here, within earshot of the fat-faced, pig-eyed, lickspittle, police-informer of a secretary.

It was enough to make a placid lump of a man angry; and Krikor Grotrian was clever and volatile. But the service of science had made him patient, and the service of the government had made him very, very careful.

He was called in by the Director at last, a man much younger than himself, whose whole air and manner proclaimed a career in the Party rather than in useful, creative work.

'Senior Research Officer Grotrian,' announced the secretary.

The Director was affable, and seemed anxious to learn.

'I see, Comrade,' he said, looking up with a smile from a folder the secretary had handed him, 'that you have been engaged on a project code-named Shemakha for almost eleven years, with facilities ... yes, and an outlay of ... yes. I see also that this project was commenced on a Directive from the Institute of Science in Moscow, to which confidential reports have been submitted bi-annually. What has taken so long, with so little visible result?'

'The brief, Comrade Director, was to develop a new strain of *Papaver somniferum*, with a high yield, a high concentration of alkaloid in both sap and straw, a high resistance to fungus parasites, and a greater tolerance of climatic and other environmental variations.'

'I am no botanist. What plant are we discussing?'

'The opium poppy.'

'Why was this area chosen?'

'The terrain is ecologically similar to those regions of central Turkey where the poppy is grown commercially.'

6

'Can you enlighten me about the purpose of the programme?'

'Yes, Comrade Director. The purpose was fully explained to me when one of your predecessors did me the honour of putting me in charge of the programme. Derivatives of opium are required medically—'

'You mean morphine?'

'Morphine and heroin. They are required medically both in the relief of severe pain and in a variety of experimental applications relating to mental illness. My understanding is that the government does not wish to import opium from major producers in the capitalist world, nor from our democratic allies— '

'Why?'

'My understanding is that the government deplores the large-scale growing of opium by backward peoples such as the Vietnamese, owing to the malignant social effects of freely-available addictive opiates among people to whom indulgence is a tradition.'

'A characteristically high-minded decision,' said the Director without conscious humour.

'Yes, indeed, Comrade Director.'

'Why does the self-sufficiency of the Motherland in regard to this important crop require the development of a new strain?'

'My understanding is that the government desires the minimum area of land to be devoted to this cultivation, and that land of minimum agricultural utility for other purposes. It is, as I understand, an exercise in the profitable use of marginal land as well as in commodity self-sufficiency. There is also, I was told, a security aspect. It will be easier to guard small parcels of marginal land against possible pilferage and misuse.'

'I understand. What have eleven years achieved in pursuit of these laudible objectives, Comrade?'

'A gratifying degree of success, Comrade Director, which evaded us until we added the cautious use of radio-active isotopes to conventional hybridisation and

7

selectivity. As you are doubtless aware, radio-activity can influence genes, so producing mutant strains of almost every living species, and under certain circumstances these genetic changes can themselves become hereditary. We now have a strain which produces thirty per cent more seed-pods, from which the sap is drawn, and under favourable conditions the pods are considerably larger, producing a proportionally greater quantity of latex. Our strain is tolerant of almost all conditions of soil chemistry, climate and altitude, and has proved itself more resistant than its parent to fungus which inhibits growth of the pod. We are also gratified to have established that the alkaloid is in higher concentration in both the latex and the straw of the harvested plants. This has been confirmed by analysis by our colleagues in Moscow. A peculiarity of the strain is that the blossoms are not white, as normally, but a variety of reds and pinks.' Krikor Grotrian allowed himself a pleasantry: 'We have developed a good Socialist poppy, Comrade Director.'

The Director laughed, seeming for a moment almost human.

Krikor Grotrian said, 'The flowers are very pretty, and resemble the annual poppies grown in gardens, some of which are, as it happens, varieties of the same species *somniferum.*'

'It is, I can understand, doubly gratifying if a new strain is beautiful as well as useful. You are near the end of your labours on this project, then?'

'Near, Comrade Director, but not yet arrived. It is necessary that the new strain should breed true, without reversion to the old. *Somniferum* is one of the annual species of *Papaver*, so that cultivators depend on seed. Clearly they should be able to harvest their own seed for the next season's sowing, but as things stand they would be dependent on us for seed. This problem has not yet been wholly solved, and now occupies our attention and unremitting energy.'

8

'You anticipate success in the foreseeable future? Or do we wait another eleven years?'

Krikor Grotrian glanced nervously at the Director. It was exactly the sort of question a scientist most dreads from a bureaucrat. But he was reassured. The Director was beaming. He was pleased with what he heard. He probably sensed that the final triumph would come during his tenure of office, and would be his triumph.

Five hundred miles to the north, in a laboratory in Volgograd (which was Stalingrad for a while, until fashions changed) two dozen guinea-pigs were injected with minute quantities of diacetyl morphine dissolved in warm water. The chemical had been synthesised from bricks of raw opium from the Institute of Agricultural Science in Tbilisi. The status of the director of the Volgograd laboratory required, for opaque bureaucratic reasons, that he conduct these tests, in order that credit for the success of Operation Shemakha should be spread more thinly.

Sophisticated analysis had revealed that the complex molecule of the alkaloid had certain minor variations of structure; it seemed possible that the effects of the heroin might be a little different, too.

They were.

The guinea-pigs went mad and died in agony.

A meeting sat round a conference table in the Institute of Science in Moscow. On the agenda was a project of long standing called Shemakha, the development of a strain of *Papaver somniferum* with certain listed advantages. It was assumed round the table that genetic stability could be achieved, as in Russell lupins. But there was a disquieting report from Volgograd about the physiological effects of the derivatives.

The scientists present were pessimistic. One even recommended immediate and permanent abandonment of the project.

The chairman of the meeting, a lay official, brusquely

overruled this suggestion. It was agreed, after long debate, conducted with an appearance of free democratic discussion, that the morphine and heroin derived from the new strain required further and more exhaustive clinical trials before final conclusions could be drawn. The chairman thus appeared, in the minutes which his superiors would see, to have presided over a wise and careful piece of scientific decision-making; in fact, like all successful officials in Communist countries, he had adroitly postponed making any decision at all.

Sergei Ivanovitch Lipotkin was an academic sociologist, studying the effects on individuals and groups of working in certain large factories. He developed his findings both in print and in lectures to his students. He reached, with apparent reluctance, conclusions which the managers of the factories found odious. The managers stood much higher with the Party than did Sergei Ivanovitch Lipotkin. He was consequently invited, one evening, into a big black car outside the gates of the university; the car drove a very long way. Officials with careful eyes told him, not unkindly, that he was suffering from overwork and loss of sense of proportion. He remonstrated, but without conviction, because he knew exactly what was happening to him.

The doctors at the Mental Hospital far away in Chelyabinsk welcomed their distinguished new patient. They were sorry that he was suffering from strain. He needed rest and treatment. He was not to worry any more.

A course of treatment was agreed upon by a conference under the chairmanship of the senior consultant. He had received two confidential memoranda before calling the conference. The first of these declared, on the highest medical authority, that the patient Lipotkin suffered from brain damage, with the consequence of severe and permanent disorientation; the good doctors of Chelyabinsk were not to delude themselves that any cure was possible, or that the patient – however rational he seemed – could ever be allowed freedom to damage himself and others. The second memorandum related to a consignment of white powder, a conventional opiate synthesised from a new source, about which further clinical evidence was urgently required.

The two memoranda determined the treatment to which the kindly, serious doctors committed Sergei Ivanovitch Lipotkin.

He was indeed suffering from brain damage before he died; but his death followed rapidly on his madness.

A general faced two staff-officers across his desk, in a building like a gigantic public lavatory in central Moscow.

The general was reading a memorandum submitted by one of the officers. It was very clearly and profession-ally set out, its author having risen in the army almost wholly by dint of submitting memoranda to generals. It followed the best models. It reported three facts, all intrinsically interesting and somewhat shocking, none likely to be known to the general, all strictly relevant; it finished with a recommendation which seemed so logic-al, so inevitable, that it could surely not be rejected. And the memorandum had been typed; carbon copies were on file; no one could claim credit except the author.

The first fact was that London alone had an estimated 6,000 heroin addicts. It was not reported as a fact, but added as a rider, that this number could be greatly increased if heroin was much cheaper on the black market; the same applied to other British cities and to cities in other Western countries.

The second fact was that pipelines by which both raw opium and processed heroin were smuggled into Western countries had been identified; they could be infiltrated, or taken over, by means of the purchase or elimination of certain criminals.

The third fact was that a new technique for the

11

production of significantly cheaper opium had been developed by an institute of agricultural science in one of the southern Republics of the Union. This product was absolutely debarred from domestic use, even in cases of extreme medical necessity, owing to undesirable side-effects.

The recommendation was that the so-called Shema-kha opium (which did not come from the Azerbaijan city of that name) be clandestinely exported in maximum quantity and at minimum price to as many Western countries as possible, with the object of creating dismay and panic, and furthering the deterioration in national fibre and morale.

The general considered the plan. Much about it was attractive. It was eminently practical, even to being financially self-liquidating.

At last the general detected the flaw for which his politically-sensitive nose had been sniffing. The ambitious little man on the other side of the desk would get no credit this time.

The general said, 'It appears to me that you are conspiring to strengthen our enemies, rather than to weaken them.'

'But Comrade General— '

'London has six thousand heroin addicts. They are a drain on resources, a visible social evil, a matter of shame and humiliation. London is weakened and demoralised by this population of useless cripples. What would strengthen London, return vitality and pride to the city? The removal of that running sore, the amputation of that cancerous toe. The quick death, in fact, of those six thousand addicts. Capitalist politicians would like nothing better, nothing, than unlimited supplies of cheap and fatal heroin made available to their addicts.'

'Yes, Comrade General,' said the staff officer woodenly, realising why the general was a general.

'However, this Shemakha substance may be useful. Anything may be useful which looks as though it would do one thing, but does another. If assassination of an addict ever became desirable, this would be a convenient weapon. For that reason a small amount of the material will be procured and kept by this Department. And total secrecy will surround the effect which it has on the consumer. Who knows about the effects?'

'A laboratory in Volgograd. A hospital in Chelyabinsk. Some individuals in the Institute of Science here. The people in Tbilisi know all about producing the material, but they have been told nothing about its effects.'

'The directorate of the laboratory and the hospital will be ordered at once that the effect of the chemical is on the Most Secret list. The secretariat of the Institute of Science will be advised likewise.'

'They want a kilo of your raw opium,' said the Director of the Georgian Institute of Agricultural Science.

'Who do?' asked Krikor Grotrian.

'The army. Presumably for the medical services.'

'Very well. I have not got it, but I can get it shortly.'

'That is one of the messages I have received today about your project. The other is from the Institute of Science. It will be disappointing to you. Perhaps you will read it yourself.'

When Krikor Grotrian read it, he felt the ground rocking under his feet and the ceiling pressing down on his head.

'I am sincerely sorry,' said the Director. 'This is not my decision, but, as you see, the order is categorical.'

'But, Comrade Director, after eleven years! ... And we are so very near final success!'

'I know,' said the Director sadly. It was hard for him, too, to be cheated out of the reward for eleven years' work, though it was someone else's eleven years and someone else's work.

'Can we not even proceed unofficially with the last stage ...?'

13

'No. That must be as clear to you as it is to me. You have read the directive.'

'But *why? Why?*'

The Director shrugged. He had no idea why. He suspected there was no reason. In his devious and careful-stepping career he had seen hundreds of decisions taken for no reason; many of them broke hearts, and some broke more than hearts. The thing was to accept orders with servile alacrity, waste no time in regrets, and set about looking for new successes to claim, new thunder to steal, or new failures to denounce.

He looked at Krikor Grotrian. The scientist's sharp Armenian face was crumpled with open misery. They were a declamatory, shameless people, thought the Director, howling like Arabs, revealing emotion like children. Some Armenians, of course, learned to affect this transparentness while simulating or dissimulating; they could be politicians of formidable adroitness, not to be trusted by an honest Georgian. But poor little Grotrian was an innocent in politics and in life. Quite likely he would be no further use to the Institute.

The depth of Krikor Grotrian's despair was evidence both of his volatile nature and of his utter commitment to his work. A rubbery resilience, a stoic acceptance, were equally outside the possibilities of his character. He brooded and raved, but always in private: though lost to all moderation of feeling, he was not lost to all instinct of self preservation.

A sensible wife would perhaps have calmed him, soothed these emotional excesses; but he had never married. He said he was married to his work, and it was true.

Brooding, he floated through waves of self-pity; he was stabbed by sharp-barbed lance heads of resentment; he was consumed with envy of men of less intelligence, less integrity, time servers who were allowed to complete their projects and to enjoy unearned celebrity.

14

Someone in Moscow was jealous of his almost-complete success with *Papaver somniferum grotriani*.

It was not he only that had been cheated, but Russia, the world. Medicine needed morphine. He had shown how to produce its raw material more cheaply, in more concentrated form, on any patch of useless land.

The more he brooded, the more a mood of defiance began to grow like a sapling in his heart: to grow, he told himself, like a firm-stemmed, proud-blossomed, many-podded plant of *Papaver somniferum grotriani*.

Eleven years' work must *not* be wasted. The world must *not* be cheated.

Still he allowed none of this turmoil to show. The assistants in the laboratory and on the experimental farms felt betrayed themselves, and showed it; but he showed nothing. Colleagues, in the cafés of Tbilisi, commiserated, showing more or less of the little nasty streak of satisfaction they felt at the destruction of a programme which might have eclipsed their own programmes; Krikor Grotrian showed nothing; he shrugged; he even smiled.

A month after he was ordered to abandon his beloved project, the time came for his annual holiday. Normally he went to sun his skinny old body at one of the popular Black Sea resorts, joyless, solitary, bored, conscientiously trying to relax, to fit himself mentally and physically for new labours. But this year, for special reasons, he went south, a hundred miles into the muddled uplands of his native Armenia. He went to Yerevan and from there, by wheezing truck, to a small village in a narrow valley where he had fourth and fifth cousins. The village was in a restricted area, only 35 miles from the Turkish frontier and 45 from the Persian; but he moved freely because he was a respected government servant. By climbing a nearby hill on a clear day he could see the perfect cone of Ararat, snow-covered, away to the south-west.

Poppies were flowering everywhere, small red weeds in the cultivated patches and at the roadsides. He was ceaselessly reminded of *Papaver somniferum grotriani*; he was not in any case here to forget it.

One night he drank too deep, at the wedding party of a distant kinsman. The unaccustomed alcohol loosened his careful tongue. At midnight he was in a most uncharacteristic position; he was lying along a low couch, his thin hair tousled and his neat moustache raffishly unkempt, with his head in the broad lap of a cousin's widow. His position, and her sympathetic nature, encouraged confidences.

He told her about his poppy.

His morning headache was not improved by the visit of an alarming stranger, a wiry, fierce-faced man of forty-five, a mountain herdsman, who insisted on taking him for a walk. He said that he was a cousin of the sympathetic widow; he had met her by chance in the Post Office; she had told him a little about a wonderful new poppy.

Krikor Grotrian was frightened and repelled by the stranger; but he realised that this was the man he had come to see. There were such men; there always had been; he himself was descended from the same stock. The Russian–Turkish frontier had moved many times, drawing different lines across Armenia. The Turks and Kurds had massacred most of the Christian Armenians on their side of the line; they and still more savage Lazes enjoyed the grazing land of Turkish Armenia. But it was all Armenia; the grim stranger knew it; he could get there, when he wanted to, in the way of business. All mountain frontiers (Krikor Grotrian knew) bred a lawless fringe of such people, herdsmen and guides and smugglers.

The mountain-man and the scientist struck up, as it seemed to the village, a surprising friendship. They spent hours in conversation, away on hilltops where nobody could hear them. They were an ill-assorted pair, but they seemed to have plenty to talk about.

They had. They were infinitely cautious with each other. They revealed themselves to one another very slowly, particle by particle, each small revelation from

16

one earning a comparable admission from the other, as though they were playing a game, or bargaining with bits of damaging knowledge. Criminals in police states have to be careful.

After a full week of sparring, Krikor Grotrian and Ara Mandikian understood each other, and had the outline of a plan.

Krikor could produce only small amounts of raw opium, owing to his situation and his commitments; in any case smuggling opium into Turkey would be like taking oil to Kuwait or ice to Greenland. But he could without detection, for a short time at least, produce large quantities of seed from which a new breed of poppy, his own, could be grown. He could bring sacks of the seed to Yerevan, on the excuse of pursuing the buxom widow. This would be credible to everyone: even creditable.

Ara for his part had contacts on the other side of the frontier, military presences notwithstanding. To one Kurdish headman whom he trusted he would give an exact account of the new poppy and its manifold advantages. This information would travel privily, from mouth to mouth, among a fraternity, until it reached poppy growers who did not want revealing cultivated fields of white blossom, but patches of innocent red weeds: and who wanted a higher yield of an opium for which more money could be charged. The opium would in time go to the ports on the south and west coasts of Turkey: but that was no more Ara's concern than Krikor's.

Krikor's eleven years would *not* be wasted. *Papaver somniferum grotriani,* rejected out of stupidity, bureaucracy, jealously, by Russia, would flourish elsewhere: it would bring happiness and prosperity to cultivators, and at length comfort to patients in hospitals.

Krikor Grotrian went back to Tbilisi and a new project, a drab little project, at the Institute of Agricultural Science.

News of the wonderful new poppy-seed crossed in due course the fertile valley of the Aras river, under the eyes of the Russian frontier watch-towers: it went by Tuzluca to Sarikamis, by Erzurum to Kayseri on the bare Cappadocian uplands. The news was welcomed by the very few who were allowed to hear it; they agreed it should go no further.

But there were ears in a coffee-shop in Eski Gümüş. A report, a little distorted, of miraculous new poppy-seed went therefore to Ankara, where it earned a little money; and from there to a carpet shop in the Great Bazaar of Istanbul, where it earned more money. The result was that, even before it began, the traffic in the new seed was part of the empire of Algan Bey, instead of being a small and tidy freelance operation.

King Jones surveyed his kingdom: a corner of a cellar in a condemned house in Battersea.

He embarked on his royal and sumptuous ritual. He mixed half a grain of heroin (bought by his Queen for a couple of quid, twenty minutes earlier, in a pub near Waterloo Station) in a few spoonfuls of water in a mug. He managed to light a match, and with the match a stub of candle. He heated the water until the tablets dissolved. His impatience, his need, became intolerable: stretched his royal courage far beyond its limits, so that he was blubbering, trembling, twitching, imploring and commanding the tablets to dissolve.

He wrapped, with scarcely functioning fingers, a filthy handkerchief round his left arm. He twisted it tight. A vein just inside his elbow stood out like a blue cord under the greasy yellow skin.

Steadying himself, the King mainlined most of the fix into the vein.

Almost at once he would feel like a king again: strong, free, capable, fearless, logical, powerful, clever, happy.

The Queen found him an hour later, dead on the wet cellar stairs. He had smashed his teeth and much of his face, trying to bite the concrete of the stairs. His body was contorted into an extraordinary position.

The Queen looked at him with dull eyes, long past surprise, long past shock, too familiar with horror to be touched by horror. She saw he had dropped the hypodermic; it lay in a corner of the cellar, by his bed, a third full. She had earned the money that bought it, pulling down her jeans for a truck-driver in the back of his truck. She was still a pretty girl, though getting very thin, and not the picture of health.

A third of it left. Pity to waste it.

'That is all,' said Krikor Grotrian on a hilltop near the village. 'There is no more. I am tired. I am frightened. The reward is insufficient. There is very little money and no glory. There are no more seeds. I came this time to tell you so. I shall not come again.'

'Ah no, my dear friend,' said Ara Mandikian. 'You do not at all understand. Were I only involved, I should be disappointed but I should accept your decision. But very many people are now involved, and a powerful man is involved. I do not know who he is, but they say his shadow reaches from Istanbul to the frontier. My life would be worth nothing, they say, if I crossed the Aras with empty hands.'

'Then stay this side of the Aras.'

'No, my dear friend. I shall cross soon, and often, with sacks of seed.'

'No.'

'But yes. I appeal to your loyalty. I remind you of our kinship and our friendship. Also I mention that the Director of the Institute at Tbilisi, a place I do not expect to visit, to my grief, will get a letter, written, perhaps, by a person more skilled at writing than I am, describing your many visits to Yerevan ...'

After a long pause Krikor Grotrian nodded. He promised to provide more seed, much more, immediately and indefinitely.

Chapter 2

'His name is Mustafa Algan,' said Hans Biebermann in his office in Zurich. 'Algan Bey. I am not sure if that honorific is bestowed by the government, an inherited title like your own, or merely the respect generally accorded to a rich and successful man, the doyen of his profession. I have met him. He came to see me, all the way from Istanbul in spite of his age, when he opened an account at this bank. That is not necessary, you understand. All a man needs to open an account with us is money, and he had plenty of that. But it is a courtesy we appreciate. He is charming, a most civilized man. His German is a great deal better than yours, my dear Sandro.'

'*Non mi piace, la tua lingua,*' grumbled il conte Alessandro di Ganzarello, sitting across the desk from Herr Biebermann.

The banker, who was no dwarf, felt as always puny in the company of his gigantic friend. Glossy and well-dressed himself, he felt a sloven when faced with the unobtrusive perfection of Sandro's clothes. Rich himself, his fortune was paltry compared to the Italian's. Clever himself, he had over many years of friendship acquired a deep respect for the speed and power of Sandro's brain – deliberately hidden, like so much of the man, behind a mask of idle self-indulgence. Only in one regard was Hans Biebermann aware that the fates had been kinder to himself. He was no beauty, but his plump, conventional features were less actively ugly than the big brown

20

face opposite. It was odd, reflected Herr Biebermann wryly, that so ugly a man as Sandro attracted so many women so effortlessly. Perhaps it was the incongruous sapphire eyes, perhaps the deep, soothing voice in which Sandro was now speaking again.

'An elderly, civilized, eminent Turkish gentleman,' rumbled Sandro. '*Simpatico, egregio,* with plenty of money. Why do you want me to look at him?'

'You are going to Istanbul anyway.'

'Yes, for a holiday. I am tired. My friends also. We had an exhausting and worrying time in India.'

'I know. The beautiful Lady Jennifer, in such danger ... But she is well now. She looked very beautiful yesterday, as beautiful as ever. She would not tell me much about your ... exploits in India. I hoped she would, but I did not expect she would. She is discreet, as discreet as yourself and the charming Mr Tucker. Even to me, who knows something about you all ...'

'You know something about us, *caro* Hans, because we know you are as discreet as we are. Otherwise you would know nothing, no more than the rest of the world.'

'That is understood, and always has been. Putting it another way, it is because I know *you* are as discreet as *I* am that I ask you to look at Mustafa Algan Bey.'

'Okay,' said Sandro. '*Di mi.*'

'He is a carpet seller, with a store in the Great Bazaar in Istanbul. He is the best of all carpet sellers. He has the best carpets to sell, and he knows most about them. That is his reputation. I sent a man to Istanbul to check. He reported that it is so. He confirmed absolutely the pre-eminence of Mustafa Algan in the world of Turkish carpets. But I was not quite satisfied. I made another investigation, very quietly, very tactfully, among the Turkish police. There is nothing against Mustafa Algan. As far as the police know, he is and always has been exactly what he seems to be, and no more. We could not enquire more closely without telling the police too much, without betraying the confidence of a client. But still we are not quite happy.'

'*Perche?*'

'Why does an Istanbul carpet seller keep his money – some of his money – in a confidential numbered account at a Zurich bank?'

'To avoid tax.'

'Maybe. But why does he have more money than a carpet seller, even the very best, could possibly earn?'

'He inherited it, from a papa who was also rich and successful.'

'Then why does it still come to us, large sums at irregular intervals, in many different currencies?'

'*Ah. Capito.*'

'If this is the Golden Horn,' said Jenny, 'I'd rather have a tin whistle.'

'The trouble with you Limeys,' said Colly Tucker, 'is you have no knowledge, no culture, no sense of history, no education, no taste— '

'Ho hum,' said Jenny, stepping with elaborate care over a dead cat on the greasy wharf. 'I think this animal had lunch at that restaurant Sandro took us to. As a matter of fact I think we ate its brother.'

Lady Jennifer Norrington attracted eyes. She did so in London and New York, even among people who did not know that she was the daughter of an earl of ancient family and large possessions. She did so particularly in Eastern countries, where her bright gold hair, cornflower-blue eyes and pink-gold skin made her as exotic and exciting as a visitor from outer space or ancient legend. The Turks were also startled, like Arabs and Indians, at her confident freedom, at the impudent equality with which she treated her men. It was shocking to the Turks, but ah! she was beautiful.

Coleridge Tucker III did not attract eyes. He attracted none in Miami or Milan, even among people who knew he had one of the largest inherited fortunes in the

United States. He looked incapable of work, decision, or connected thought.

His disguise was as good as Jenny's.

The water of the Golden Horn was crowded with elegant caiques, bustling ferries, fishing boats and dinghies. Through half-closed eyes it was possible to see romance and beauty. But if you opened your eyes you saw that the caiques were slovenly, the ferries ramshackle and overcrowded; and the most famous stretch of water in the world was dirty, cloudy with pollution, full of unspeakable floating objects.

'Well, it's something I had to see,' said Colly defensively. 'My relatives said, "Boy, go walk along the historic Phanariot Shore of the Golden Horn." I have some very, very highly educated relatives, and I have to report for debriefing when I get home. They're gonna say, "Boy, did you walk along the historic Phanariot Shore of the Golden Horn, like we said?" Now I can say, "Relatives, I did. Scout's honour." '

'Having done it, we can stop doing it?'

'Yes, darling.'

The trip to Turkey was pure holiday. That had been clearly understood by both Jenny and Colly. It was earned by a time in India which was not a holiday at all. The trip was suggested by Sandro, who knew the country a little and wanted to see more of it. Jenny Norrington had accepted immediately, because accepting Sandro's invitations (all but one) was the pattern of her life. Colly Tucker accepted with reluctance and foreboding. 'From what I hear from my educated relatives,' he said, 'the whole place is littered with relics of bygone civilizations, and my educated relatives are gonna require me to examine every last goddam one.' But the lure of an entirely new country was as strong to Colly as to Jenny, and his army of deeply serious kin, who united in deploring his frivolity, would have been surprised at the crash course in Turkish which he took in New York before he left.

The trip was pure holiday. Yet Sandro seemed to have things to do, people to see, questions to ask. He rumbled apologies and disappeared for hours at a time. Jenny and Colly shrugged to each other.

'Is that a sleuth face the big lunk has on,' asked Colly, 'or some other face?'

'I don't want to hear about it,' said Jenny. 'I don't want to think about it. Let's go and see where they murdered what's-his-name.'

Jenny had had enough of Istanbul after a week, though she found the pervasive sense of the past strong and fascinating. In the one-time harems of the Topkapi Palace it was easy to feel the luxury, cruelty and intrigue of the degenerate Ottomans; the Ahmet and Suleiman mosques were deeply impressive; but filth and squalor, poverty and stench lay only just behind the most resplendent façades. Jenny found it a city with too many dead cats and too many live cockroaches.

It was a holiday, but Sandro was up to something, and in the end Jenny asked him about it.

'There is a man called Mustafa Algan,' said Sandro, 'who sells carpets in a shop in the Great Bazaar.'

'You need carpets,' said Colly. 'Okay, buy goddam carpets. Do we have to hang around here indefinitely while you make up your stupid mind what carpets to buy?'

'Maybe I buy a carpet from him. He is a great expert and, as a carpet seller, of unusual honesty in this city. That is well known. It is very good cover, you see, the best possible.'

'Bloody hell,' said Jenny. 'There you go again. Colly was right about your face. Cover for what? I suppose he's the Napoleon of Turkish crime. I suppose you're going after him. I suppose you want us to come too. Well, I won't do it.'

'Me neither,' said Colly, without conviction.

'I do not know cover for what,' said Sandro. 'He is maybe a very big fence. He is maybe quite clean.'

24

'Oh great,' said Colly. 'Great, great. He keeps a carpet store as a cover for being clean. I guess it's so unusual in this city a guy feels self-conscious about it.'

Sandro told them about Hans Biebermann's perplexities. 'If Hans is holding millions of dollars of stolen money,' he finished, 'he wants to know about it.'

'Why does he?' asked Jenny.

'Because Hans is an honest man.'

'Honest he may be,' said Colly. 'But he's pretty indiscreet. He can't have any of my business, if he's gonna tell every fat Wop layabout he meets how much dough I send along.'

'Hans is only a very little indiscreet,' said Sandro, 'and only to me, and for a good reason.'

'Only to you is right,' said Jenny. 'He didn't say anything to me about it. So he doesn't want me to hear about it. So I don't want to hear about it. I want to go down the coast to look at the goats.'

'You think he's a crook,' said Colly, 'just because he earns a surprising amount of moo and banks it in Zurich instead of here?'

'It makes a possibility.'

'Okay okay, go look at the store.'

'I have looked. It is just a store, with very fine carpets. Mustafa Algan is away, he is in Cappadocia buying carpets from the families who make them, or who made them a long time ago.'

'You're saying he has a perfectly legit operation,' said Colly.

'Yes,' said Sandro. 'He is what he seems to be, a lover of carpets. I do not know if he is also what he does not seem to be. Bundles of carpets go into that store, rolled up, from every part of Turkey. They go out again, they go all over the world. People come into that store, rich people from every country, American, Italian, German, Dutch, Swedish, Brazilian, Japanese. To nearly all of them he can talk in their own language. They give him cash, or a traveller's cheque, or a cheque on a local bank.

That is for a carpet. The money goes into a bank in Istanbul. Do they give him also, for something else, a dollar cheque made out to the number of his account in Zurich?'

'Well, it seems they do,' said Colly, 'only we don't know why. I don't *want* to know why, but Hans Biebermann bought me a drink a few years ago, and I guess I have a favour to return. Do we peek at the rolled-up carpets going into the joint?'

Sandro frowned. Jenny thought he was going to suggest burgling the carpet shop in the night, when the Bazaar was locked and silent. The thought scared and excited her.

'No,' said Sandro. 'I have found out some things, and spent some money. That is what I have been doing this week. Somebody else will pull the fire out of our chestnuts. Is that right? A truck is coming in from Kayseri, with carpets, to the store of Mustafa Algan. I know the number of that truck and its route. The police have been tipped off that there is *contrabanda* in the truck, rolled up in the carpets. Stolen goods, currency. They will search. Maybe we solve all the problems of Hans Biebermann without getting our feet wet at all.'

Jenny felt a mixture of disappointment and relief.

She said, 'Couldn't Hans have done this himself? Why bother you?'

'Hans has a different education,' said Sandro gravely. 'He is expert at banking. I am expert at getting phoney underworld tip-offs to the police.'

'No good,' said Sandro.

'The cops didn't catch the truck?' asked Colly.

'Oh yes. It was where we thought it would be, at the time we thought it would be there. It was full of carpets, rolled up and tied with string. The police unrolled every carpet. They searched the truck, and the driver, and the friend of the driver. Then they shook hands, and apologised very much, and went home to bed.'

'That's that, then,' said Jenny. 'One of us three has made a colossal nit of himself, and it's not me, and it's not Colly. Can we *now* go and look at the goats?'

'I think there is a leak,' said Sandro equably. 'After I tip off the police, a person in the police has tipped off the firm of Mustafa Algan. So the truck was clean. Nothing is proved. Next time we will not tell the police, so there will be no tip-off to Mustafa Algan, so maybe the truck will not be clean. Always I guess this will be necessary. If Hans is right about Mustafa Algan, if he has grown very rich without anybody knowing, and without any official suspicion, then he has bought protection. At least he has bought regular information from inside the police department.'

'It figures,' agreed Colly reluctantly.

'It figured always,' said Sandro. 'Always I expected this, that to find anything we would have to find it ourselves.'

'Then why,' asked Jenny suspiciously, 'didn't you say so before, you devious Wop? Why did you say the bluebottles would pull the firenuts out of our chests for us?'

'I thought you would be angry. I thought you would think this was a bastard's vacation.'

'I'm not so sure it isn't,' said Colly.

'Busman's holiday?' suggested Jenny, used to some of Sandro's wilder jabs at colloquial English.

'*Giusto.*'

'I wonder what a busman is,' said Jenny. 'A driver? A conductor? But I don't wonder very hard. And I don't wonder what a harmless old carpet seller has inside his carpets, either. I don't want to hear any more about it, and I don't want to hijack a truck and unroll a lot of bloody carpets on the road.'

'Yes, you do,' said Sandro.

Jenny never knew the full extent of Sandro's contacts. They were remarkable. He had not an address-book but a library of address-books, and all the entries in all the books were not so much individual persons as gateways to armies, telephone directories, employment agencies, encyclopaedias of local knowledge. Sandro collected contacts as other people collect honours, match-covers or money. Armed with them, he could arrive in a country he did not know well, like Turkey, and within days could become the intimate of friends of friends of friends, at the highest and lowest levels of society, among government departments and petty criminals.

Jenny guessed he spent a good deal of money. It bought him information and a wide variety of services. The information, this time, stopped short of anything firm about Mustafa Algan, except the negative, interminably repeated: there was nothing known against him, he was clean, he was a great man among carpets – no more. Either this was the truth, or his arm was long and his power formidable. There are whispers about almost every eminent man. There were none about Mustafa Algan. This was in itself remarkable. The more so, since there was a lot of money that could not be explained in a numbered account in Zurich.

Sandro could get no whisper, from bankers or bureaucrats or burglars, about any illegal activity of Mustafa Algan. But, at a lower and more practical level, there were things he could find out: such as the numbers and makes of small trucks bringing carpets to Istanbul, their routes and times and stopping places. These things were not difficult to find out, because they were not secret. The innocent transport of innocent carpets across Turkey was done in broad daylight by respectable men. The only trick was in getting the information without seeming to get it. Without, above all, becoming identified as a man interested in these matters. As well as information, Sandro could get such things as the vehicles he himself needed. Still he was not identified. The man who hired the truck for him was the friend of a friend of a friend; he had never seen Sandro;

he did not know his name or that he was a foreigner.

Sometimes Sandro's machine made life easy for his friends. Sometimes dangerous. Sometimes both.

Early in the morning they put a hired car on the boat at Galata. For three hours they chugged across the smooth sea of Marmara to Mudanya, and drove off the boat into a different world. They were in the south; it was Asia, not Europe, although the feeling was strongly Mediterranean. They crossed a soft, teeming plain of vineyards and olives, fruit trees and maize and tobacco and regimented poplars, dominated by the snow-capped magnificence of Mysian Olympus, one of the homes of the ancient gods.

They looked down on Bursa from the terrace of a restaurant on a spur. Everything was brightly coloured, all the houses washed in yellows and reds and a bright sky blue. The town was full of gardens, vines, trees, which flowed over walls and roofed the cobbled alleys. Part of Jenny wished they were here for a peaceful reason. Part was taut with excitement.

They drank coffee on the terrace after lunch. Sandro inspected the marvellous view through binoculars. It was a reasonable thing to do. Many tourists did it.

'*Eccolo*,' he murmured, handing the binoculars to Jenny.

Outside the town, on the main road from the west, there was a small roadside café. Beyond was a track leading up into the hills, which disappeared behind a row of close-planted cypresses. A big cattle-truck had turned off the road. It was crawling up the track. It stopped behind the cypresses, a hundred yards from the café.

'Is it big enough?' asked Jenny dubiously.

'Yes.' said Sandro. 'But with nothing to spare.'

Jenny handed back the binoculars. Through them, Sandro saw the driver of the truck cross a small orchard from the cypresses to the café. He went into the café. It

29

did not matter what he said, because he knew nothing. Presently he would stroll into the town and take the bus to Eskisehir. All this had been arranged by a man who did not know what he was arranging, beyond the delivery of a hired cattle-truck to a place just outside Bursa.

The café had one window which looked out onto the open space in front where cars and trucks could be parked. Sandro had been told, by a man who knew the café, the size and height of the window. Looking through the binoculars, he thought that his informant had exaggerated the size of the window, and the extent to which it commanded the car-park. That was a good thing, although he was not pleased to have paid for inaccurate detail.

It was to be hoped that the other information he had bought was more authentic. If so, Mustafa Algan's van was now in the area of Karacabey, fifty miles to the west, collecting a number of carpets. It would come to Bursa some time during the evening. The driver would spend the night there before going on to the ferry and to Istanbul in the morning. He would stay at the café, not as a client but because his cousin owned it. He did so whenever possible, whenever his route lay in this direction. This was public knowledge, insofar as anybody was interested in the habits of an obscure middle-aged driver. The van would spend the night outside the café, locked and under bright lights. It was in the last degree unlikely that anyone would attempt to steal any of the carpets in the van. They were high-quality pieces, and therefore distinctive. They could be described by Mustafa Algan so that any expert would recognise them. It would be exceedingly difficult to offer them for sale anywhere in Turkey, and equally difficult to smuggle them abroad.

'But won't they be extra careful,' said Jenny, 'after the police searched the other van?'

'Maybe,' said Sandro. 'But the police said that other

search was a mistake, a misunderstanding. They were full of apologies. It is not likely Mustafa thinks he is suspected by the police, because he is *not* suspected by the police. He does not know that anybody else suspects him. He does not know that Hans has a friend like me.'

'He knows *somebody* tipped off the police, even if he believes them that it was all a mistake.'

'Yes. Maybe they are careful. That is why we are being very careful also.'

Later in the afternoon an ox-cart plodded, among many others, towards Bursa from the west. This one turned into the space in front of the café. Colly watched it through the binoculars. The driver backed the cart against the front of the café, against the one window which gave onto the car park. He unharnessed his ox and led it away. If there were objections he ignored them.

'Another arrangement?' asked Colly.

'*Si*. It cuts off the sight from the window. Also, Mustafa Algan's truck cannot station himself in that exact place, just outside the window. It must be somewhere else, *not* just outside the window. You know, it was more trouble and expense to arrange that little cart than to arrange for the big truck?'

'I hope the ox gets a cut,' said Jenny.

Not long afterwards they got into their car and drove northwards from Bursa. A few people saw them go. Their departure, if anybody asked about it, would be remembered, because Sandro and Jenny would be remembered.

Sandro drove north towards Mudanya and the coast of the Sea of Marmara. After a few miles he turned left onto a little road, and left again onto a track which took them southwards. He had been assured the track was motorable; it was, but only just. He joined the road between Karacabey and Bursa a few miles west of Bursa. He parked inconspicuously behind a disused barn. They waited until full dark. They had a bottle of wine and a

31

picnic. Only Sandro was hungry, but Colly and Jenny
drank some of the sweetish local wine. In the dark they
drove to the edge of Bursa. Sandro stopped two hundred
yards short of the track up into the hills, in which the
cattle-truck was parked.

'*Andiamo*,' he said.

They got out of the car and walked up the track to the
cattle-truck. There was nobody about. The night was
dark. Sandro used a pencil flash cautiously on the track.
They could hear music from the café. The lights outside
the café were very bright, to give security to the vehicles
parked there.

Sandro checked the tail-gate of the cattle-truck. It
seemed strong. Inside, the back of the truck smelled of
diesel oil and dung. Jenny wondered again if it was big
enough.

Sandro found the ignition key of the truck under the
rubber mat for the driver's feet, where he had arranged
for it to be left. Colly got behind the wheel of the truck
and started it. The noise of the engine was tremendous
when he revved it; it sounded like the engine room of a
ship with every rivet loose. Colly began to back the truck
down the track to the road.

Sandro and Jenny walked across the orchard to the
café, as the truck driver had done. They stopped short of
the brightly lit area in front of the café. The ox-cart was
still resting in front of the window, obscuring it. There
were two vans, two cars, and many bicycles outside the
café.

Jenny glanced at Sandro. He pointed to the larger of
the vans, a Ford fifteen-cwt, anonymous, no trade-name
or insignia painted on its flat green sides.

Sandro prowled to the green van, moving with
extraordinary delicacy for a man of his bulk. A radio
was playing inside the café and there were subdued
voices. A wild party would have been better, but the
party in the café was not wild. The radio was not loud.

Sandro picked the lock of the van's back door. He

opened one side of the double door and peeped in. Jenny stood guard, out of sight but able to see. Sandro blinked the beam of his flash inside the van. There were long cylindrical bundles stacked so as half to fill the van: carpets. There was a grunt from the darkness, a movement, a snore. A man was asleep on the stack of carpets, locked in the back of the van.

They were being careful.

Sandro switched off his flash and softly closed the door. It could not be opened from inside. No communication was possible between the man in the back and the driver in the cab of the van. The man in the back had ventilation but he could see nothing. He could attract the driver's attention by banging on the metal which divided them. Conceivably he had a speaking-tube. He was not neglecting his duty by going to sleep, because no carpet could be pulled from the back of the van without waking him. He was undoubtedly armed. He had a gun and probably a flashlight, both under his hand as he slept. It made a complication, but one which Sandro's plan took into account.

Softly, with Jenny standing guard, Sandro picked the lock of the driver's door of the van.

Colly drove the cattle-truck slowly and noisily to the front of the café. The engine thundered and the truck vibrated. He lined up the truck with the carpet van, and backed it to within two yards of the van's radiator grille. The noise of the truck was an ordinary noise in this place.

Jenny pulled out the pins from the tail-gate of the cattle-truck, keeping watch as she did so. She lowered the gate, which made a steep ramp from the ground to the floor of the truck. The ramp was slatted with wooden battens, so that cattle going in or out did not skid on the sloping metal.

Sandro started the van and drove it up the ramp. He woke up the man inside the van. The man shouted and banged on the metal walls of the van. His shouts and bangs, and the van's engine, were drowned by the thunder of the cattle-truck's engine.

The van nosed forward, then stuck. It was fractionally too high to fit inside the cattle truck. Sandro had paid for another piece of inaccurate information.

'All we needed,' said Jenny, inaudible under the cattle-truck's wheezing thunder. She wanted to run away and get into the hired car and drive very fast in any direction.

Sandro, in the driving seat of the van, pointed at its wheels. He made a jabbing gesture. He called out something, but Jenny could not hear him. After a baffled half-second, Jenny got it. She let the air out of all four tyres of the van.

Sandro crunched into bottom gear again. He roared the van's engine and inched forward and up. The flat tyres just made the difference. The roof of the van scraped against the inside of the cattle-truck, but the van inserted itself into the truck. Sandro went forward until the front of the van clanged against the wall of the truck.

Jenny struggled with the ramp. It was too heavy for her. Sandro jumped out of the van and helped her. They locked the tail-gate in place with the pins. Colly already had the truck moving by the time Jenny and Sandro scrambled into the cab. Nobody came out of the café to investigate so ordinary a noise as the roaring of a heavy truck's engine.

Colly turned on to the road and accelerated away to the west. He slowed as he passed the place where Sandro had parked the hired car. Sandro jumped out of the truck and ran to the car. He started it, and followed the truck for three miles. He flashed his headlights as a signal to Colly, who pulled off the road and stopped. Sandro stopped behind him.

'Hey,' called Colly from the cab of the truck, 'lights!'

Sandro jumped out of the car and ran to the front of the truck. He made an urgent gesture of silence as soon as Colly could see him.

'Well, okay,' said Colly softly. 'But there isn't anybody for miles, and I didn't make so very much noise, compared to this leviathan here— '

'You have a passenger, *caro*,' said Sandro.

'Why sure. Blonde cookie I picked up outside a café. What her momma would say if she knew the kid was hitching rides with a truck-driver— '

'In the little truck. A guard for the carpets.'

'Oh. Ah. Yeah. See your problem. You might have mentioned it before. If he hears us talking English, and knows it's English, and we don't happen to kill him ...'

'I don't think we ought to do that,' said Jenny. 'Unless we have to. And I don't see why we should have to. We're not doing anything we care about so very much, are we? Just prodding about for Hans Biebermann. If he wants people killed, let him come and do it.'

'If we let down the ramp,' said Colly to Sandro, 'your lights glare right at the ass of the little truck, right?'

'That is why they are on.'

'Sure. So when we open up the back of the little truck, the guy inside is gonna be like skewered by those headlights, and dazzled, and helpless, and he won't be able to see us, so a tone of sharp command ...'

'We tell him to come out,' said Sandro. 'I think he comes. We hit him on the back of the head.'

'I suppose we might go that far,' said Jenny dubiously.

They arranged themselves. Colly stood beside and just behind the headlights of the car. (Sandro's bulk, even in such a position, might be visible and remembered.) Sandro and Jenny stood in the truck each side of the tail of the van. Colly and Sandro both had guns in their hands, Jenny a cosh. Sandro twisted the handle on the back of the van. He and Jenny pulled their doors wide at the same moment. The car's headlights filled the inside of the van.

Colly blinked at what he saw. The man inside had been busy in the short time the van had been inside the truck. He had shifted some of the carpets so they lay across the van, forming a massive bulwark. He thought a few big rolled carpets would stop a bullet. He was right. Colly saw him, fleetingly, behind his parapet of rolled carpets. It would be possible to shoot him there, but it would not be easy. It would not be agreeable, either. It would be simple murder.

In Turkish, in an assumed gruff voice, Colly called, 'Out'.

The response was fast. There were three crashing reports from behind the barrier of carpets. They were shockingly magnified by the confined space, by the metal sides of the van. Bullets crashed into the headlights of the car, smashing them. A third bullet slammed close to Colly's shoulder, between him and the car. It hit some projecting piece of the car; the riccochet droned away across the dark countryside. Colly ducked into cover behind the car.

It was bottomlessly dark after the glare of the headlights. There was no sound from the man inside the van.

Sandro's brain raced. This man was an extremely fine pistol shot, and he was brave. To shine a flashlight at him would be to get killed. If the man moved quickly and quietly, he could be out of the van and out of the truck before they knew it. He could be away in the darkness. There would be no chance of catching him. He could run for help. He'd know exactly what had happened to him. Several cars could be hunting for a big cattle-truck within a short time. Or he could wait around, safe in the darkness, to see what they did. They could pull the carpets out of the van and unroll them in the road, but there could be no real search without a light. If they used a light he could kill them. He could also, with more shots from that very accurate gun, completely disable the car and the cattle-truck.

The man had not jumped out yet. The urgent thing was to stop him doing so. Sandro slammed shut his side of the double door, knowing that Jenny would understand and do the same. She did. Sandro dropped below

36

the level of the tail of the van and reached up to turn the handle. He risked being shot in the arm through the thin metal of the door, but it was not a huge risk.

The man was locked in the van. But they were locked out of it. They could abandon the operation, cut their losses and quit. But they could not go fast or get far, in a dark night, on strange roads, in a car without lights. The disappearance of the van from the café might by now have been noticed. It might have been reported to the police. The police would not at once see the van in the cattle-truck, if the tail-gate was closed, but they would be highly likely to search the cattle-truck. How would three foreigners explain their presence, if they were found anywhere nearby? Why, if they broke the head-lights of their car, did they not walk a few miles to the comforts of Bursa? If anybody did come by, the man inside could declare his presence with one shot. Time was on the man's side. Dawn made a search of the van impossible, in this populous countryside, even if the man was dead or not there. Dawn meant alarm and search parties, even if there were not already alarm and search. By dawn the three of them must be well away from here, far from van and carpets and cattle-truck. And the man must not have seen them, or heard their voices, unless they were prepared to kill him and could find a way of doing so.

'I think,' said Jenny softly, 'It's what they call stalemate, don't you?'

Chapter 3

They went well away from the truck, so that they could talk freely without the man hearing their voices or language.

'One thing to do,' said Colly, 'is get way the hell off this big road, so if a bunch of squad-cars come screaming along they don't find us standing around with egg on our faces.'

'I can drive this car without lights,' said Sandro, nodding, 'if I follow your lights.'

'The dumb leading the blind,' said Jenny.

'Drop dead, you Limey cow,' said Colly. 'Speaking of dropping dead, I have to point out that if we really want to break this stalemate, we can do it quietly as we drive along.'

'*Si*,' agreed Sandro.

'You've thought of something I haven't thought of, then,' said Jenny.

'It is easy,' said Sandro. 'We start the motor of the little truck inside the big truck. We close up the big truck, cover the ventilators. We leave the motor of the little truck to run, inside the big truck ...'

'Exhaust does the rest,' said Colly. 'Stuff called carbon monoxide.'

'Oh,' said Jenny. 'Oh no. Oh no no.'

'Well, baby, he tried pretty hard to kill me. It's a thing I can't forget about him, try as I may.'

'He was doing his job. He was guarding those bloody carpets.'

'Is that how they guard carpets in this goddam country? Throw slugs at anybody who happens by?'

'I think he is guarding more than carpets,' said Sandro.

'That's what I figured,' said Colly. 'He must be. So I got all curious. I wasn't all that interested before, but I am now. It's amazing how a bullet six inches from the old ear-lobe sharpens a guy's intellectual curiosity.'

'As a matter of fact,' said Jenny, 'I admit I'm a bit curious too. Not very. Only a bit. So we can give him just a little whiff? Enough to make him woozy? Like dentists used to?'

'No,' said Colly. 'It's impossible to guess how long that trick would take. We might just send him off to sleepy-byes in half an hour. We might kill him in that time. Or that amount of exhaust-fumes might have no effect on him at all, sealed up there inside that little tin box. Then, when we all climb in as happy as rabbits, he blasts large holes in our heads from behind that wall he made.'

'I know,' said Jenny. She frowned, tapping her teeth with a fingernail. The others waited, looking at her, knowing that her suggestion might be absurd, or excellent, or both.

She said, 'We tip him out. We undo the back. We don't open the door, just undo it. Then we lift up the front of the van, and tip it further and further backwards, until the whole lot just slides out with a whoosh. Carpets, him, his gun, everything. Then we jump on his head. I mean you do. Then we unroll anything you want to unroll.'

'Tip,' said Colly. 'How?'

'I don't know. That's just mechanical. You work that bit out. I've done the difficult part.'

'The truck must have a big jack,' said Colly. 'Big enough to lift the bows of the van way off the ground. We prop it like that, put the jack on some kind of platform, jack up some more— '

39

'Maybe high enough to put the front wheels of the van on the back of the truck,' said Sandro. 'Then reverse the truck …'

'Up and up and up she goes,' said Colly. 'Yeah, it could work. I never saw it done. But then, I never met this particular problem before. If we weren't so goddam squeamish we wouldn't *have* a problem. I still think … okay, okay, I don't really want to gas the guy to death. Only a part of me does.'

Colly drove the cattle-truck far up a path between fields of towering maize. Sandro followed in the hired car. They stopped. They lowered the tail-gate of the cattle-truck. Sandro got under the wheel of the van and reversed it down the ramp. They found the big jack used for changing the wheels of the cattle-truck. They chocked the rear wheels of the van. Very gently, Sandro twisted the handle of the van's rear door, so that it was closed but unlatched. With the jack under the front of the van's chassis they raised the van's nose effortlessly until the wheels were a foot clear of the ground. Other tools from the truck, jammed in endways, held it in this position, rather precariously, when they pulled the jack clear. Rocks raised the big jack so that it could lift the front of the van a further foot. The process was repeated. Presently the front wheels of the van were higher than the rear bumper of the cattle-truck. They closed the tail-gate of the truck. Colly started the truck and inched it backwards. The tail-gate of the truck took the weight of the van. Very slowly, nursing the heavy clutch, Colly continued to back. The van's front wheels began to climb vertically up the tail-gate of the truck. They went up and up, until the van was at forty degrees.

Then it happened. The rear door of the van burst open. The cargo of rolled carpets slid downwards and outwards. Those lowest in the load slid only eighteen inches before the ends came to rest on the ground. The higher ones had a yard or four feet to slide until their lower ends met the ground. A few small rugs, rolled as tight as the carpets, were tipped clear out of the van. There was no sign of the man, in the beam of Sandro's flashlight.

Crazily, Jenny wondered if he had somehow got out and run away.

Colly continued very slowly reversing, so that the front of the van climbed higher and higher. The man was holding onto the upper ends of the rolled carpets, which were still well inside the van. He could do this until the van was vertical.

Sandro wondered what would happen if Colly changed gear and drove sharply forwards. The van would crash to the ground, landing the harder for having no air in the tyres. The man might be killed or damaged. But, clinging to the carpets and protected by them, he might be perfectly all right. Then they were back where they started. What would happen if he tipped the van right over on its back? The man would scarcely be undamaged then. It was odds against his being killed, but there was a clear chance of a fatal accident. Sandro shared Jenny's squeamishness about three of them killing one brave man who was doing what he was paid to do. He knew that, whatever he said, Colly shared it too.

Suddenly the dilemma was solved, the stalemate broken. Three carpets crashed down out of the back of the van into the beam of Sandro's flash. They were not lying longways, like the rest, but across. They were carpets the man had used for his barricade. They had been jammed across the inside of the van, then the man's weight and the angle of the van had shifted them. They thumped down, three together, onto the dirt of the path. The man was in the middle of them. Sandro jumped on him. But he was already unconscious, stunned by the fall, maybe by the impact of a heavy rolled carpet landing on top of him. He was not dead. He had maybe broken a collar-bone, or been concussed.

He was a small, stringy man with a toothbrush

moustache. He wore shabby grey trousers and a dark jacket, and a woollen shirt buttoned to the neck without a tie. He had a knitted cap, which had fallen off his head. His gun was a Luger. He also had a big sheath-knife, a razor, and a club with a lump of metal on a whippy fourteen-inch handle of plaited leather. Sandro guessed he was as good with knives and club as he was with the gun, and he was very, very good with the gun.

They could blindfold him if he returned to consciousness. Meanwhile he was harmless.

With the carpets, a surprising amount of dirt had poured down out of the back of the van. It sprinkled itself onto the tumbled carpets, and over the clothes of the unconscious man. There were small drifts of it on the dry earth. It was a kind of dark dust, gritty.

'What is this stuff?' asked Jenny. 'It feels like bird-seed.'

'Maybe keeps out the moths,' said Colly. 'Keep your eye on the ball, baby, will you please?'

They cut the cords that bound the rolled carpets, and slit the sacking that wrapped them. They unrolled all the carpets. There was nothing in the carpets. There was nothing in the van, front or back, or in the pockets of the little man who had done so well trying to do his job.

'I suppose,' said Jenny, yawning over a late breakfast a long way away, 'I've spent a more pointless and idiotic night. Yes, I remember. Once. It was when I was three. I stayed up all night to meet a ghost. She was called the White Prioress. I never did see her. That was a sensible and well-spent night, compared to last night.'

'We have learned something of importance,' said Sandro.

'You have? I certainly have. I've learned that never again, under any circumstances, am I going to be induced to spend my nights, or my days, or any part of my days— '

42

'We have learned,' said Sandro calmly, 'that Mustafa Algan employs professional heavies to guard his loads.'

'So do half the companies in England,' said Jenny. 'Ever heard of Securicor?'

'We have learned that whatever Mustafa Algan does, he does not bring things into Istanbul inside carpets. At least, not always.'

'And that's important?'

'Yes.'

'You're pleased you found that out? It made your night? You're all rosy-cheeked and triumphant?'

'Of course. It was very necessary to know. The great fortune in Zurich comes to him another way. Now we must find that other way.'

'You find it,' said Jenny. 'I'm going to look at goats.'

'I am very sorry,' said the stringy man with the toothbrush moustache. 'I can tell you nothing about them at all. I did not see the car or the big truck. I did not see the people. I only heard one voice, saying one word. I do not think I would recognise the voice. Oh yes, there was one thing strange. There was a boy with them, a young boy with a high voice. I heard him cry out, just one little cry. I do not think I would recognise that voice, either. One young boy sounds like another. I thought it strange that such people should bring a child with them on such an operation. Perhaps it will help us, but I am afraid it will not help us very much.'

'Who knows?' said Mustafa Algan. 'A young boy with a high voice. It is a thing to bear in mind. The English, at one time, used young boys for burglary, because they could go through drainpipes and windows too small for a man. A book called *Oliver Twist* describes the method. I recommend it to you. Of course, I read it in English, and it may lose in translation ... Something is going on I do not like.'

'All the seed was lost.'

'All?'

'All but a handful. A wind came up in the dawn, and blew twenty kilos of seed over the fields.'

'I wonder how much of it they took. I wonder if they took any. I wonder if they know what it is. Yes, of course they know, and of course they took some. It must be so. And now we must be even more careful than usual.'

Sandro received a message that Mustafa Algan was back in Istanbul. He said he would go to the Great Bazaar after lunch, to look at carpets and at Mustafa Algan.

'By all means, darling,' said Jenny, gesturing languidly.

'You will come too. I want to know what you think of this man.'

'Hopeless. Colly and I are having lunch with Princess Thingummy.'

'Come after lunch.'

They went, of course. Their car was driven with unceasing though illegal blasting of the horn, among thousands of others equally clamant; all the drivers steered where they saw gaps, regardless of rules or of lines painted on the streets. The car swerved and screeched towards the enormous grey mosque of Süleyman the Magnificent, whose dome and minarets dominate the skyline of the old city, and dwarf the huge area of the Bazaar into shabby insignificance.

'Originally the Royal Mews,' said Colly in a guidebook voice. 'Same like that place behind Buckingham Palace, only bigger.'

'The mosque?'

'The Bazaar, stupid. I thought you'd be interested, seeing as how you're practically always climbing up onto goddam horses and falling off them again.'

'You're wrong, darling. Wrong about me falling off, and even wronger about me being interested. Is that the outside of the Bazaar? Just a blank wall. No doors. We can't get in. We can't go and look at Sandro's carpet seller. What a pity.'

The driver stopped at the mouth of a side-street; he pointed to an arched doorway into the Bazaar.

The noise outside, in the street, was almost unbearably loud: the roar of traffic, screech of brakes, blare of horns, shouts of drivers, thin screams of ragged children perilously playing obscure games among wheels and feet. When they went through the doorway into the Bazaar this outside noise was blanketed by the ancient walls, and drowned by amplified music, the shouts of pedlars, the gabble and babble of business also conducted at a shout because of the noise. The inside din was just as loud as the outside, but more congenial. It was difficult to move among the dense crowds and the urchins and old men selling things; it was easy to get lost. The Bazaar was a maze of little crooked streets and alleys; it seemed a whole town, enclosed and roofed, with Post Office, banks, mosques, restaurants, brothels, innumerable coffee and tea shops, and distinct quarters for various trades. Jenny liked it.

Consulting a piece of paper on which Sandro had drawn a diagram, Colly steered them at last to a plate-glass window in a side alley, in which hung a single carpet of great beauty.

'Fine piece of map reading,' said Colly, 'in pretty difficult country.'

'If all this was really stables,' said Jenny, 'the horses must have died of old age before they got out.'

'I'm a stupid American,' said Colly by the door of the shop, 'looking for something to impress the folks back home with.'

'I should think they'd believe you,' said Jenny.

Jenny preceded Colly into the shop. A smooth, respectful man hurried forward at once, not quite rubbing his hands. He looked at Jenny. He saw the mane of bright hair, a little dishevelled after the furious drive and the milling crowds of the Bazaar; the face, pink-gold from the sun, a little too round and snub-nosed for perfect beauty but of breathtaking prettiness,

45

illuminated by large blue eyes which gave an impression of friendliness but not of much intelligence, and lent a touch of enchanting absurdity by a dimple – not two, but only one – in the left cheek; he saw, and correctly interpreted, the blue cotton dress whose simplicity did not hide its excellence, the expensive bag and shoes. These last might have been American, but not the dress; the hair might have been Swedish, but not the pink-gold skin.

The salesman said, in English learned in Britain or from a Briton, 'Good afternoon, Miss, are you interested in looking at some of our carpets?'

Colly came in. The salesman looked at him also. The salesman, in neatly pressed pants and shiny black shoes, in clean white shirt and silk necktie, was a million times smarter than Colly. Colly looked a mess, a hobo. He wore baggy khaki pants, grubby sneakers, a short-sleeved shirt faded by sun and salt water to a sort of psychedelic cloud effect; his green eyes blinked self-deprecatingly from an unremarkable face; a thatch of mouse-coloured hair looked as though it needed not brush, comb and scissors, but garden rake and lawnmower. All this the salesman saw. But he saw something else, which a less experienced judge of customers would have missed.

What he saw encouraged him to say, in English learned in America or from an American, 'Good afternoon, sir. Do you have any particular interest as to date or region, or shall I show just the best we have right now?'

Colly said, 'Show us something good but small, and when you show it tell us *why* it's good.'

The salesman produced prayer-rugs from Konya and Gördes, and a very old one from the now-discredited area of Kayseri. He explained that they were good because of the quality of wools and silk they were woven from, because the colours were natural, traditional vegetable dyes, because in the workmanship there were few knotting flaws, because the designs were unusual in

46

detail but characteristic in feeling. He expanded all these points, giving a lecture in traditional carpet making in glib and fluent Anglo-American. He mentioned prices, which seemed to Jenny astronomically high. The rugs were beautiful, but she did not need rugs, and could not possibly have afforded any of these rugs; her attention went from the rugs to the salesman.

She was sure this was not Sandro's man. Without being obsequious or humourless, he was somehow an unmistakable employee; he might do all the selling in the shop, but he did not own or run it; it was no fortune of his, clean or dirty, that went to a bank in Zurich.

Jenny wandered away from the impressive technicalities of the salesman. Through a small arch she saw another room behind, the walls ablaze with carpets. Sandro was there, examining with another man a large carpet of wonderfully rich, dark colours. They were deep in conversation; neither paid any attention to Jenny.

The two were in almost ludicrous physical contrast. Sandro towered over his companion; his immense chest and shoulders threatened as always to burst out of his jacket. In his big ugly face, deeply tanned after their months in India, eyes as brilliantly blue as Jenny's own were more than usually incongruous; silver watch-springs were scattered through the tight black curls of his hair. (There was much more grey in Sandro's hair, Jenny had noticed, than before the tension and despair of India; there was new grey in Colly's mousey hair, too, although he was well under forty; it was because they had both thought, there in India, that she was lost to them for ever.)

The man who was showing the carpet to Sandro was tiny, like a little silver bird. His face was aquiline, pale skin drawn tight over high cheekbones, a narrow high-bridged beak of a nose, rapid black eyes, thick white hair, carefully brushed, giving almost the effect of a crest; his thin white hands fluttered as he talked, gesturing, emphasising, pointing; he had a light voice, a high tenor, in contrast to Sandro's deep rumble; the Italian he was speaking was as fluent and almost as correct as Sandro's.

Apart from the language they were using, one thing only was common to the two men: the excellence of their clothes, perfect in cut, expensive in material, faultless in taste. Sandro's suit, like all his suits, was English (he always wore a dark suit in a city, no matter what anybody else wore; Colly, who was several times richer, was believed not to possess a suit at all). Jenny thought the little birdlike man's suit was English, too; she did not think Savile Row could be imitated in Istanbul, any more than the miraculous carpets could be imitated in Halifax or Axminster.

A little, dapper, birdlike man, with fluttering hands, and a fluting birdlike voice, and expensive English clothes, and a command of languages: was he a fence or a gangster? He looked incapable of sustaining the weight of an ordinary pistol, utterly incapable of frightening an ordinary Turk.

Another man came into the room from a further curtained archway. There was much more of the shop than Jenny had realised. The newcomer was a little younger than Colly, a little older than Jenny – perhaps thirty. His features were regular and pleasant, his clothes respectable but a little shabby; he looked a professional man, intelligent and essentially serious; Jenny thought he might be a doctor. He started self-effacingly across the back room, as though not wishing to disturb the boss and his spectacular customer: but the little birdlike old man put out a hand to restrain him (it could not, by force, have restrained a mouse) and said something in Turkish. Jenny thought it was a friendly, conventional farewell. The young man nodded and smiled. Jenny, a critic of smiles, thought he had a nice smile.

He was still smiling when, coming towards the front part of the shop, he saw Jenny. It was with her so

48

instinctive to smile back that she was scarcely aware of doing so. She then remembered the Turkish rules of behaviour and morality and of the place of women, and turned away to listen to Colly and the salesman. It appeared that Colly had undertaken to buy a rug, perhaps more than one, and that a price would presently be agreed between them, somewhere above or below 10,000 Turkish lira.

There was a sudden shuffling noise, an exclamation, and Jenny was buffeted in the small of the back. She staggered, but kept her feet. The young man with the nice smile had tripped on a corner of half-unrolled carpet; he had nearly fallen, nearly brought Jenny down.

His apologies, in fair English, were profuse. 'That was nearly a very great disgrace,' he said, 'I am so extremely sorry.'

Jenny said it was nothing, that no harm had been done, that she was not hurt from the small nudge he had given her. But nothing would stem the flood of his apologies, nothing remove from his face the anguish of contrition. What restitution could he make? How could he atone? Would the English lady be restored by tea, or by coffee?

Jenny realised she was being picked up. She thought he was doing it rather nicely. All the rules of Turkish life forbade her going alone, with this stranger, even on so harmless an expedition as one to the tea shop three doors away: but conversation between them, well chaperoned in the carpet shop, was both possible and desirable.

Jenny gave the predictable replies to the predictable questions. No, she had not visited Turkey before. Yes, she was much interested in everything she had seen. Yes, she had seen the Topkapi Palace and the Blue Mosque. Yes, they would be going down the coast to see the ancient cities and temples of Lydia and Caria.

'And the goats,' said Jenny. 'To tell you the truth, I like goats better than temples.'

49

The young man did not believe her, but he found the joke exquisitely funny. He laughed at the remark much more appreciatively than it deserved. It was part of his technique of picking her up, and a perfectly acceptable part. It was all much better than the fatuous assumption of conferring a favour, to which she would have been subjected in Rome.

By this time Jenny knew that the young man was called Şefik Bozkurt, that he was an engineer, that he lived with his family at Izmir (which she discovered was Smyrna) where he did too much work for too little money, that he was in Istanbul for a short trip which combined business with pleasure, that he had hoped to buy a carpet from Algan Bey for his mother but the price of all the carpets was too high for him, and that she and her friends would be welcome, at any time, to visit his family, who saw too few interesting strangers.

Jenny preferred houses and families to hotels and hotel servants; she liked lifting lids and looking behind closed doors; she was never content to speed along highways, but always wanted to stroll off down lanes or alleys; she liked the cheerful and modest Şefik Bozkurt; she said that they would all most certainly come to visit his family in Smyrna.

At this point, simultaneously, Sandro emerged from the back room and Colly from his haggling with the salesman. A porter followed Sandro, carrying a sausage of rolled carpet of enormous length and weight; Colly had two small rolled rugs.

Jenny performed introductions. Coffee was proposed. Şefik Bozkurt was included in the party. He dined with them also, at a restaurant which he recommended. They sat after dinner on a terrace overhanging the Bosporus, warm and companionable, drinking innumerable cups of powerful coffee and smoking aromatic cigarettes. Şefik struggled to contribute his share to the cost of the dinner: he was not free-loading. His manners were in fact excellent. He could laugh loud and long without

50

loss of dignity; he could argue hotly without disrespect or bumptiousness. He expected to be in Istanbul for a few more days, and he was delighted to have found congenial company.

'He's delighted he found you, baby,' said Colly to Jenny, when they got back to the rickety palace Sandro had borrowed.

'And I'm delighted I found him,' said Jenny.

'Don't break the poor kid's heart for him.'

'No. I don't want to do that. I like him.'

'*Anch'io*,' said Sandro unexpectedly; Jenny had thought he was asleep.

'Is your carpet seller a crook?' she asked him. 'I didn't ask before because of my boyfriend.'

'What did you think, *carina*?'

'He doesn't look strong enough to be a crook.'

'He is as strong as the people he hires, if he hires such people to do other things than guard valuable carpets in small trucks ... I shall tell Hans Biebermann that I think Mustafa Algan is a crook, but I do not know what sort, and I am not going to spend any more time and money trying to find out. This is *not* a bastard's vacation. *Ecco*.'

They stopped outside a shop window full of silk from Bursa, made from silkworms fed on the mulberries of the sacred Mysian Olympus.

'I do not want all the silk in the world,' said Şefik Bozkurt to Jenny, 'But I want some of it. I work, I pay what I must pay for my parents and for their doctors, and there is no money left for silk. Did you see the Street of the Goldsmiths, in the Great Bazaar? Did you see the jewels? I do not want all the carpets sold by Mustafa Algan, but I want some.'

'For your mother.'

'Yes, for her. There is a very great debt I would like to repay, a debt I owe my mother. For myself also. I am not so *very* greedy, but I would like a few good carpets in

51

a house of my own. I could go to Germany to work. I would work not as an engineer, but as a man watching a machine in a factory. I could make plenty of money and bring it home.'

'That would be horrid.'

'It would be wonderful, but it is impossible, because of my parents. I am sure you will like them, when you come to Smyrna and visit us. I am sure they will like you too. My sisters also, although you will surprise them. You will see, when you visit us, why I cannot leave. So' – he grinned, to show that he was not being too self-pitying – 'no wife, no house, no silk, no carpets. Sandro Bey has one more carpet than he had yesterday morning. Where will it be? Does he live in a great palace?'

'Well, yes,' said Jenny, thinking with a kind of home-sickness of the Castello di Montebianco asprawl on its crag in the foothills of the Italian Alps.

'A palace full of marble and silk carpets. He has a wife?'

'Not now.'

'But he has you.'

'No. Not in the way you mean.'

But Şefik did not believe this. Comradeship between man and woman, so close and so long-established that it resembled twinship or marriage, was utterly outside his imagination. Şefik thought Sandro was Jenny's protector because their relationship was close and because he was a rich European nobleman.

'I,' said Şefik, 'make you a promise.'

'Oh dear. Do you think you should?'

He laughed. But Jenny saw that he was serious when he said, 'I shall be rich also. Not with a marble palace, I admit. But with comfort and freedom.'

'Good. How will you manage that?'

'By growing poppies,' said Şefik.

Chapter 4

'At the Gümüş Palas?' said Mustafa Algan to a thin dark man in a gaudy shirt, who had scuttled into the carpet shop delivering a package of tie-on labels. 'Şefik Bozkurt? Are you quite sure? How can he pay for dinner at the Gümüş Palas? Even I find it extremely expensive.'

'He did not pay. He was with a very large man who looks like a black bear with blue eyes, and an American whose clothes offended the head waiter, and a fair girl who did *not* offend the head waiter.'

'Şefik Bozkurt met those foreigners by chance, Algan Bey,' said the carpet salesman. 'He appeared greatly struck by the English lady, and contrived to talk to her. Thus he met the others, her friends, and they went away together.'

'The Italian asked me questions,' said Algan Bey thoughtfully, 'like a man well accustomed to ask questions. A short time afterwards he bought dinner for Şefik Bozkurt at a very expensive restaurant. Did they meet by chance or by design? If by design, by whose design? Did Şefik Bozkurt contrive to talk to the girl, or did she contrive to talk to him? There is something here I do not like. I want Şefik watched as long as he is here, and I want him watched in Izmir. I want the foreigners followed. If they go to Izmir and see Şefik again, I want to know exactly what happens. There is something here I do *not* like.'

'There is another matter that I must report to you that I think you will not like, beyeffendi,' said the thin

53

man in the gaudy shirt. 'One of the storemen in Izmir, named Kemal, has started, quite recently, to take a small quantity of morphine.'

'One of my storemen?'

'Yes, beyeffendi.'

'He is taking my morphine?'

'Yes, beyeffendi.'

'Morphine from what source?'

'It is part of the consignment made from the legally-grown opium of which we, ah, borrowed a truckload in Sivihisar three months ago.'

'Oh yes. Not our best. Not as good as the new consignments, from the new Russian poppies. Nevertheless this is intolerable. You are quite right to report the man to me, and quite right that I do not like it. It is and always has been a strict rule of this organization that theft and consumption of the product is punishable by protracted death. It is a rule I have extremely seldom been obliged to enforce. It must be enforced now.'

'The man has been in your service for thirty-five years, beyeffendi.'

'Then he should know my rules.'

'He has six children.'

'Then his family responsibilities should make him more careful and more virtuous. What kind of example is he setting his sons, stealing from me? Times are difficult enough as it is, without our legitimate profits being reduced by pilferage by our own staff. The rule must be enforced *pour encourager les autres*, as the French amusingly say.'

'The value, beyeffendi, is scarcely— '

'The value is only a small part of the point. Even if the wretch paid me for the morphine, the sentence would be the same. I cannot permit my employees to become drug addicts. The security risks would be frightful. That is not a point I need to labour. The safety of all of us, of the whole operation, depends on the reliability at all times and under all circumstances of all our employees. Once a man takes drugs, on no matter how demure a scale, he ceases to be reliable. The world knows that. Also, the scale becomes progressively less demure, which the world also knows, and which is a fact fundamental to the success of our business. Really I am disgusted. Addiction is a terrible thing. Men become animals. They destroy themselves. It is a most shocking thing. I entirely subscribe to the policy of the Turkish government in this regard. I do not agree with the government in all things, but I wholly agree with them in my detestation of drug addiction. They try to forbid it throughout Turkey, and succeed fairly well. I try to forbid it within my organization, and I succeed very well. That success depends entirely on the enforcement of my rule. Remember, the man's death is to be protracted, and I do *not* want it to be a secret within the organization.'

The ship was small and elderly, but quite comfortable. It left Galata at sunset, chuffed all night the length of the Sea of Marmara, and in the morning called in at Gelibolu, once called Gallipoli: a fishing village under a castle. Grass had grown over the old Turkish coastal batteries; but there were rockets with atomic warheads, invisible in underground bunkers. The officers of the little ship, knowing Jenny was English, boasted politely about the great victory of their armies over those of the British Empire.

The sea had narrowed into the Dardanelles; presently the Dardanelles narrowed into the Hellespont, swum by Leander for Hero and Byron for a bet. Jenny, talking to a middle-aged American party, convinced them that Hero was a man, as the name suggested, and Leander's love-life of a colour all too typically Grecian. She said Byron's club foot was really a webbed foot, which was how he swam the Hellespont so quickly.

None of them noticed a neat, shabby Istanbul business-man who followed them on board at Galata, sat near them in the saloon, leaned on the rail when they did, and made apparent calculations in a little black account book.

They left the ship at Çanakkale, on the Asian side of the narrows; with the necessary permits which Sandro's contacts had secured, they solemnly inspected the excavations of Troy.

'There's Mount Ida,' said Colly, 'where the guy picked the first Miss World.'

'And this,' said Jenny, 'is where Helen's bedroom was.'

'How the hell do you make *that* out?'

'It's the place I would have chosen, and I'm supposed to be descended from her. It's got the nicest view.'

The view was the plain where the Greek armies had camped beneath wild fig trees, tamed now into farmland, irrigated by Homer's Scamander. Jenny tried to imagine the ships drawn up on the sands at the lip of the plain, and the wind-blown dust raised by the wheels of the war-chariots.

'I can almost hear the horses of Achilles neighing,' said Colly romantically.

'No, darling,' said Jenny. 'That's a goat bleating.'

They joined another ship, for the next leg of their leisurely journey down the Aegean coast. It was a little larger. The deck was thick with labourers going home to their villages, sleeping or smoking placidly on tattered rags of bedding, smelling pungently. They were bringing back money they could not earn at home. Jenny thought of Şefik Bozkurt, longing to get away from home, to earn money to buy beautiful things and to buy freedom, but the prisoner of his duty to his parents.

Jenny made friends with a family of shy Turkish children; she made animals by tying knots in handkerchiefs; they gave her a Turkish lesson. Colly looked at the anfractuous coast-line and the gusty, tricky winds with a yachtsman's eye; his Turkish was stretched beyond its limits by a technical conversation about navigation with one of the ship's officers. Sandro slept.

None of them noticed the neat, shabby businessman, who had waited for them at Çanakkale and followed them on board their new ship.

The ship threaded the narrows between Lesbos and the mainland, then delivered them at Ayvalik. A car took them to Pergamum, a fortified city magnificently placed on a crag between two rivers.

'These people,' said Colly, who had been ostentatiously busy with an archaelogical guidebook, 'once had the second best library in the world. What's more, they invented books. I mean, things with pages, instead of something wrapped around a stick like a towel in a public john.'

'What a rotten thing to invent,' said Jenny.

'Antony gave the whole lot to Cleopatra.'

'How sweet.'

'And then somebody burned them.'

'Quite right.'

Their boat had lingered to unload irrigation pipes and oil-drums, and load produce from the rich, crowded farmland of the coastal river valleys. They rejoined it after two days. They did not notice the neat, shabby man who, if he was on business, had plenty of time for it.

They docked at Smyrna during the night – Izmir, since Atatürk massacred most of the Greeks and pushed the rest into the sea. Jenny woke up to find they were almost in a noisy and crowded street running along the waterfront. Carts, trucks and buses honked to and fro; darting among them, barefooted dockers carried crates on their backs from warehouses to the dockside. In the harbour there were ships from many countries; Jenny was amused to see an American and a Russian freighter jammed side by side, their crews inspecting each other with unflattering curiosity. A crowd of pimps and pedlars had assembled on the dock; they were waiting for the American sailors to come ashore.

A dark-suited, respectable figure crossed the street

57

from a shipping office; he walked along the waterfront towards Jenny. He saw her, almost directly above him in the stern of the boat. He waved and laughed: it was Şefik Bozkurt.

'How did you know we were on this boat?' shouted Jenny over the noise of the traffic and the babble of the dockers.

'I did not know. I have met every boat.'

Jenny was flattered but worried. She remembered Colly's unneeded warning. She was under no illusions about herself and her effect on people. She was a girl men fell in love with, not all but some. Sometimes she fell in love with them, too, and sometimes with men who were not interested in her at all, or who despised her apparent vacuity, her apparently aimless and sybaritic life. She liked Şefik Bozkurt but there was no chance at all that she would fall in love with him. This was not because loving him would be unwise, purposeless, futureless; she had loved before unwisely and futurelessly. It was just because it was so. Şefik was an attractive man, a nice man, but he lit no fuse in Jenny, set no strings thrumming.

But his feelings were another matter. It was in Jenny's mind that they should leave at once, not disembark even, pass up the tomb of Tantalus and the other marvels Colly promised them from his guidebook, go far away; that she should see no more of Şefik.

But somehow, before she could put this to Colly and Sandro, the four of them were having coffee in a shop overlooking the desperately tidy Kültür Park in the middle of the town: and they had accepted an invitation to visit Şefik's family.

There was no secret about the invitation. It was not whispered. It was announced in English and then, as practice for them all, in Turkish. Colly replied in Turkish. Jenny was still worried, but she nodded and smiled. Every word of the conversation could have been heard by anyone in the shop who was interested. A neat, shabby businessman from Istanbul did not appear to be interested. He made a note in his account book, perhaps recording the outlay on his cup of coffee. Evidently his business was here: but he still had plenty of time for it.

He made a telephone call to Istanbul from the Post Office.

The Bozkurt family and their house seemed, at first, entirely modern and western; this appearance was misleading.

The house was a modern villa, half way up Mount Pagos, in a street of others: part of the suburban sprawl which has completely covered the city refounded by Alexander the Great. It made Colly think of Los Angeles, Jenny of Gerrard's Cross, and Sandro of hell.

Şefik's parents matched their house. The father had been a merchant; he spoke good German and some English and French; he wore a shabby dark suit like Şefik's, with collar and tie and neatly polished little black shoes. His clothes suggested that he was still busy in office or warehouse, but he had suffered some kind of nervous breakdown, and was now incapable of action or decision in any but the smallest domestic concerns. Şefik's mother wore dowdy, respectable middle-aged clothes in which there was no trace of Asian taste; she was severely crippled with arthritis, and walked painfully with the aid of a rubber-tipped stick. There were three girls, all much younger than Şefik, who wore cotton dresses and nylon tights and costume jewellery. The effect they all combined to give was of the most banal European middle-class household.

The first difference the newcomers noticed was in the attitude to hospitality. The Bozkurts' house, and everything in it, was instantly the property of Şefik's friends. The daughters all hurried to the kitchen where they remained, heard but only intermittently seen, for several hours. Şefik's father poured glasses of raki, and one daughter or another appeared with interminable trays of coffee. The middle daughter performed traditional dances to divert the guests (Şefik said that her respectable gyrations were on no account to be confused with belly-dancing) while the others pressed pasties on Colly and Sandro and refilled their glasses and coffee cups.

Jenny was treated with politeness, but she was not important. Only men were important. Şefik allowed himself to be waited on, hour after hour, by his crippled and hobbling mother. It was obvious to Jenny that the mother was just as happy with this arrangement as Şefik was; she was just as outraged as her husband when Colly got up to help one of the girls with a heavy tray. It was clear that round Şefik, normally, the household orbited, now that his father was no longer capable of active life. He was not only breadwinner but also king, and his male guests enjoyed all his royal privileges.

But it was also clear that for Şefik, especially after a few glasses of raki, everything orbited round Jenny. There was no mistaking the looks he gave her, the way he hovered round her, the way he constantly tried to have a private conversation with her in the midst of the family hubbub. It was unfortunate. His mother looked distressed and angry and confused. As the hours wore on, nobody being permitted to leave or to stop eating and drinking for a moment, Şefik's sisters continued to come in from the kitchen with dishes of stuffed peppers and vine-leaves, of aubergines and sardines, of apricots and sweet cakes; these were pressed on Colly and Sandro, and after them on Şefik and his father; and by Şefik they were pressed on Jenny; and his mother did not like it at all.

Jenny thought she understood. Obsession with herself was the worst thing that could happen to Şefik. At best it could only make him more restless, more bitter that he could not get away from home to make a lot of money in Germany. It could only pull him outside the tight, protected, traditionalist circle of the family, subject him to the exotic and dangerous influences of the decadent Christian West.

60

Jenny followed the older woman's eye and process of thought, which was easy because the mother was not a subtle personality. The eye rested, dark and troubled, on Sandro. Sandro was himself looking at Şefik with a frown. Jenny, seeing this, knew he was only concerned about Şefik, whom he liked. Şefik's mother might interpret the frown in quite a different way. She might think it was possessive jealousy. These respectable, educated, suburban people were not likely to go always armed as the men of the interior did: but they were not unlikely to react with the utmost ferocity to the infidelity of their women. They were rigidly conservative, rigidly possessive, and they had a tradition of personal vengeance. Şefik's mother would think Sandro felt the same way: it was a part of manhood, and he was very much a man.

Every moment that went by increased Şefik's enslavement, Jenny's embarrassment, and Şefik's mother's fear that Sandro might be goaded into a crime of vengeful violence.

Yet the laws of traditional Turkish hospitality insisted that the party go on and on, with more spicy food and raki and coffee, more music on the old stringed *sas*, more dancing from the stolid middle daughter, more attempts at intimate murmurs from Şefik, more frowns from Sandro, more fears of disaster in the old lady.

The unassuming businessman from Istanbul was relieved at midnight by a local colleague, a man who looked like a wrestler. The wrestler would watch the villa until dawn. It was highly disagreeable, but it was an order from Algan Bey.

Şefik said again to Jenny what he had said to her in Istanbul. He would not become as rich as Sandro Bey, or live in a palace full of marble and the finest carpets: but he would be a lot richer than he was now. He would look after this father who had become terrified of the world outside his house; and his mother who was

61

inconvenienced by arthritis to a point that interfered with her performance of household duties; and these obedient and virtuous sisters; and there would be money to spare for travelling, and for a house of his own with beautiful things in it; and one day for a pale-haired wife.

After much raki, Şefik said he knew it would be difficult to take Jenny from Sandro. Sandro had claims on Jenny – had, perhaps, paid her father a lot of money for her – and he was a very rich pasha. But he, Şefik, would soon be able to offer Jenny many things he could not offer her now.

'Poppies,' said Jenny in the morning. 'He's going to get rich growing poppies.'

'Opium,' said Sandro at once. 'There is a legal Turkish industry and an illegal one. The illegal industry smuggles raw opium in bricks, mostly to Marseille, where it is turned mostly into heroin.'

'Could there be any other explanation?'

'No.'

'No. Oh dear. He's not so *very* greedy, you know. He just wants a few things he can't afford.'

'Every criminal in history has said just exactly that same thing,' said Sandro.

'Yes, I know,' said Jenny. 'But this is the first one I've liked. I think I'd better go and see his poppies.'

'Why, *cara*?'

'Just on the offchance you're wrong.'

Şefik denied that he had mentioned poppies, either in Istanbul or in his father's house. He said that he could not possibly grow opium poppies anywhere near Smyrna, which was thickly populated and visited by many tourists, as they were easily recognizable.

Jenny nodded sadly, seeming to believe him but not doing so. She wondered where he could hide a crop of opium poppies. They were, as Şefik said, instantly recognisable because they were invariably white.

'I thought you said we ought to go away,' said Jenny.

'Yes,' said Sandro. 'Now I say we must stay a little. Remember when we first saw Şefik Bozkurt?'

'He was trying to buy a carpet.'

'He said that. He was in the shop of a man who earns too much money, and puts it in a bank in Zurich.'

'Well, yes. But I thought you said you weren't interested in that man any more.'

'I was not. My interest has maybe come back. I would like to see Şefik's poppies, which will make him rich enough to buy you.'

'To buy me what?'

'To buy you.'

'Oh, I see. Not very nicely put, but I'm afraid that does sum it up. That's why I want to go away. Look, why don't Colly and I go away, further south, and you can join us when you've finished hunting for wild flowers?'

'No, *carina*, as you know very well. He has already given himself away to you, two times, after drinking too much, and he will do so again. You are the hold we have over this man. And he is an interesting lead to Mustafa Algan in Istanbul.'

'Yes darling, I know all that, but what you don't understand is that it's absolutely horrid to be the hold you have over someone. I don't *want* to be your hold over anyone. It's sort of cheating. It's a rotten way to treat love. It makes me feel an absolute bitch.'

'*Capito.* I understand that it is horrid. It is also horrid to export the opium that turns into heroin that is pushed in Milan and Paris and London.'

'An exporter. Is that what he is? I suppose anybody here is well placed to export the stuff.'

'Yes. The customs are good, you know, and I do not think that Turkish officials take so very many bribes. But the Turks do not mind so much what opium goes out of Turkey. They are very, very strict about the use of drugs in Turkey, and importing of drugs into Turkey,

63

but a lot of farmers live by growing opium illegally, as well as the ones who grow it legally. If Şefik smuggles illicit opium out of Smyrna, in foreign ships, that explains how he is going to be rich, and why he was in the shop of Mustafa Algan, and why Mustafa Algan has millions of dollars in Zurich.'

'All beautifully simple and tidy. Why not tell the police?'

'Tell them what? What do I know? That Şefik talks about poppies when he has drunk too much raki? That he goes to look for a carpet for his mother in a famous shop of carpets?'

'That Mustafa Algan has a lot of money in Zurich.'

'You know I cannot tell the police that. I would be in very bad legal trouble and Hans Biebermann would be broken.'

'Then you'll just have to scrape up a few facts, darling.'

'Yes, that is exact. That is why we will stay here and why you will help.'

'Bloody hell,' said Jenny. 'Why can't I keep my big mouth shut?'

Şefik wanted his three new friends to come and stay in his family's house for an extended period. It was quite natural that he should produce this idea and press it. The rest of the family, more surprisingly, added impassioned demands of their own to his repeated invitations. Their rules of behaviour obliged them to. It would have been a thoroughly bad idea. The Bozkurts' house would have been uncomfortably crowded, and Şefik would have had many opportunities for unchaperoned contact with Jenny, which Turkish rules allowed (idiotically, she thought) in private though not in public. Although he wanted this contact, it would have been hard on him, and quite hard on Jenny too.

Sandro was able to extricate them from going to stay

64

with the family, inventing other friends who were expected to join them. Jenny, watching Şefik's mother while Sandro made his speech of polite refusal, was sure the old lady thought Sandro was protecting his concubine from her new admirer. If anything, Jenny thought, it was the other way about: with the qualification that she had never quite allowed herself to become Sandro's concubine, for a thousand good reasons, although with a certain regret.

Meanwhile Şefik took every moment that his job and family spared him to be with Jenny and one or both of the others. He did not mention poppies again. Insofar as he courted Jenny, it was with a curious mixture of traditional male arrogance and pathetic humility. Jenny understood the origins of both feelings, and was very sorry for him. More than ever she wanted to go away, because to offer him any hope was cruel.

But Sandro's criminological antennae were quivering, and he would not go.

'If Şefik Bozkurt intended to betray Algan Bey to the foreigners,' said the man who looked like a wrestler, 'he could have done so ten thousand times by now. I think they are all friends, and the friendship is innocent, and we are wasting our time.'

'Do not say so to Algan Bey,' advised the little businessman from Istanbul.

'I would rather die quickly than do so, because if I did so I would die slowly.'

'Yes. As slowly as you yourself caused Kemal the storeman to die, for stealing Algan Bey's morphine.'

'As slowly as that.'

'Kemal's screams, I think, were heard from Gelibolu to Hakkari, from Izmir to Trabzon.'

'That was Algan Bey's intention. His death was to be silent no more than it was to be speedy. I do not think any other person will eat Algan Bey's morphine until it has been sold far away in a foreign city.'

'I should hope not,' said the little businessman primly. 'To take such drugs, except in case of medical necessity, is a weak and degraded folly.'

It was Colly whom Sandro principally used to keep an eye on Şefik. This was because Colly, though a pale-eyed mouse-haired foreigner, was inconspicuous even in a Turkish town. He had the gift of hardly being wherever he was. A friend of his in New York said that Colly made a room emptier by entering it, fuller by leaving it; he did not realise how great a compliment he was paying to Colly's skill.

Colly did not precisely tail Şefik: that *would* have been impossible. He did not know all the people Şefik talked to in his office in the port. He did know that Şefik's routine fitted absolutely with his job in an engineering company and his heavy family responsibilities.

Şefik had many friends in Smyrna, educated young middle-class men like himself, whom he presented to the foreigners. He was proud to do so; made a point of doing so. There did not appear to be any close friend or colleague that he kept hidden from them. But it was impossible to be sure about this, or to have any idea what Şefik and others said to each other in private.

'They are watching him also,' said the little businessman from Istanbul.

'Ah,' said Algan Bey on the telephone.

'Not all the time but much of the time. The American. I must tell you that he is an expert. If I were not also an expert I would not have noticed this.'

'If you were not an expert you would not be in Izmir now, or in my employ. I wish I knew who these people are and what they want.'

'Can you not – I ask with respect – find out who they are?'

'I have found out all about them, and it is nothing. The Italian is a rich noble who likes pictures and women. The girl is noble also, and likes horses. The American is very rich indeed, and likes only yachts. They are all well known to hundreds of people. To millions, as they all have their photographs in newspapers. But all this is not the whole truth about them. We know the American and the large Italian are experts. I think the girl is expert also; I think she contrived to make friends with Şefik Bozkurt when he thought he was contriving to make friends with her. They may be doing business with Şefik or they may be spying on him. They may be running with the gazelle or with the greyhounds. If he is doing business with them he is betraying me. If they are spying on him, he will probably betray me. I should ask you to kill him now, but that would make them suspicious if they are not already suspicious. It is an annoying situation. Supplies will be coming to Izmir soon and my pipeline must be open. Şefik is ideally placed, sufficiently greedy, and tied to Izmir by his family. I do not want to replace him unless it is necessary. I do want to know more about his friends. You will continue to observe and to report, with extra staff if you think it necessary.'

Far away to the east in the little drab town of Sille, on the bleak central plateau of Anatolia, a man straightened from a laboratory bench. The bench was in a high, well-lit room in a house which was much larger than it seemed from the rutted back-alley on which it fronted.

The man was young. He looked educated, almost refined. He looked out of place in this dingy little settlement in the wilderness. He looked bored and dissatisfied. He was alone in the room. He prodded absently with a spatula at a heap of white powder in an enamel dish. A furtive look came over his face, a look of curiosity, hunger, guilty excitement.

His hands were trembling as he measured a small amount of the powder onto a sheet of clean paper.

The door opened. Another man came into the room,

an upright elderly man with a big moustache and a fierce eye. He saw the piece of paper with the white crystals in a tiny pile. He saw the guilty, greedy face of the younger man.

'No!' he barked. 'If you are going to do what I think you are going to do, you will anger Algan Bey and you will be punished accordingly. Have you not heard of a man named Kemal, in Izmir?'

'He was seen, Fikret,' said the younger man. 'I shall not be seen, except by you, and you would not betray your own nephew.'

'Mustafa Algan sees everything,' said the older man. 'He punishes everything.'

'You are old-fashioned and superstitious, Fikret. Even Mustafa Algan cannot see me here, now, in this room with a closed door and shuttered windows, five hundred kilometres from Istanbul.'

'I tell you that he can, and that you will be punished.'

'By you?'

'There will be no need for me to punish you. Algan Bey will do it.'

'You think he has magical powers, like the djinns our fathers believed in. I think he is an employer who keeps me in this unspeakable place and pays me too little money. I am not going to become an addict, you know. I am motivated by curiosity. I am a sort of scientist, after all. I work with these materials. I produce quantities of this chemical. I know that it has an enormous value, that people steal and kill for it, but I do not know *why*. I am intensely curious. I cannot bear to go on, performing this repetitive and ill-rewarded task, without experiencing, just once, what the miracle of this stuff is.'

'I warn you solemnly.'

'Just once.'

'You will regret this bitterly and for ever.'

'Just once, Fikret!'

The young man grinned lop-sidedly. He raised the paper, and before the older man could stop him he

68

poured the white powder into his mouth. He waited a moment, with an expectant air, as though angels were about to sing inside his head.

Suddenly his face was contorted into a horrible, unrecognisable mask, the mouth stretched wide, as though he had been struck by intolerable pain. He began to smash his head downwards onto the laboratory bench, into the glass and porcelain and enamelled metal. He smashed the glass with his face. Blood poured over the bench. He had no face. He was screaming out of a mouth which was no longer a mouth. He sank to his knees on the floor, faceless, smashing what had been his face into the woodwork of the bench.

He was dead within four minutes.

A truck arrived later in the day to the house in the back alley. Fikret told the driver and the two men with him what had happened to his nephew.

'Algan Bey's eye is keen and his arm is long,' said the truck-driver, awed.

The driver and his friends carried the news, in whispers, north into Cappadocia, and then south to the Mediterranean coast. It spread, still in whispers, all through the empire of Mustafa Algan.

'We can wait here until we grow long white beards,' said Colly, 'without learning any more than we know.'

'If I grow a long beard,' said Jenny, 'it won't be white. I'll dye it green.'

'We can't search his house,' said Colly. 'It's always full of people. I suppose we could search his office one night.'

'If we found a ton of opium there, we couldn't pin it to Şefik,' said Jenny. 'Dozens of people work there, and most of them look like murderers.'

Sandro said, 'I know Şefik's exact salary, because I have got myself an introduction to the *direttore* of the firm, and I go to talk to him about business. I know how much money Şefik must pay for the house, for food and electricity, and how much for the doctors. He has no savings out of his salary, not one lira. Yet he went to the most expensive carpet seller in Istanbul, the very best. To buy a carpet, as he said? That is not possible. He had another reason to be there, which he lied about. I am now certain that Mustafa Algan is a very big man in drug smuggling, and that Şefik Bozkurt is a small man in it. It must be so. It answers all questions.'

'Okay, you're certain,' said Jenny. 'I'm sorry to believe it, and I don't think I do believe it, but even if you're right, what are you going to do about it?'

'Anonymous tip-off to the cops?' suggested Colly.

'No,' said Sandro. 'They could do nothing except search and ask some questions. That will simply warn the other side. We must find out the truth.'

'How?'

'We have tried to do it in a clean way, by watching and waiting. Now we must do it the dirty way. You, Jenny *tesoro*, must find out from Şefik how he is going to be rich enough to buy you from me. It is reasonable that you should want to know. If you are in love with him, you want to know what is your future. You must make a decision. You can only make it if he tells you some facts. *Capito, cara?*'

'*Capito.* Kaput. I won't do it,' said Jenny.

'This is *drugs*. The most evil of all crimes.'

'No. To pretend to fall in love with Şefik, in order to stab him in the back – that would be the most evil of all crimes. Delilah got a lousy press, if you remember. I won't do it.'

Sandro saw that she would not. He knew no argument would budge her. He said they must go on watching and waiting, and if Colly wished to grow a long white beard he could do so.

They took a hired car to the so-called Lake of Tantalus, who was condemned to eternal thirst because he served up his son, boiled, to the gods for dinner.

Şefik came with them, as he did whenever he could.

He was not much interested in classical myth, but he wanted to be with Jenny. He had never heard of the Lake of Tantalus.

They drove round the bay to Karşiyaka, then inland and up the dry slopes of Yamanlar Daği, part of the Mount Sipylus of the ancients. The road was quite good as far as the Yamanlar Sanatorium. Then the car bumped another five twisting miles of very bad road, climbing almost to the summit of Yamanlar Daği.

Suddenly Şefik said, 'We are going to Kara Göl.'

'Yes,' said Sandro.

'I did not realise. You said a different name. Of course I know Kara Göl. The water is very deep and cold.'

'It was once a city,' said Colly, 'according to a guy called Pausonius.'

'Impossible!' said Şefik.

'I have to believe somebody, chum, and I choose to believe Pausonius. There was a fine marble city, only an earthquake destroyed it, and made a hole in the ground, and the hole filled up with water.'

'No, no,' said Şefik. 'That is quite impossible. There is nothing there to see, no temple or statue, no theatre, graves, nothing, only just trees and water. I do not think you want to see it. Truly it is not interesting. Let us go to a different place.'

Sandro, driving, caught Jenny's eye. He saw understanding in it, and dismay. Şefik did not want them to go to the Lake of Tantalus.

A battered jeep followed them, well behind, driven by the man who looked like a wrestler. He was bored but conscientious. He had driven scores of miles in the jeep, following the foreigners to the petrified remains of Niobe, eternally weeping, to the Karabal pass with its Hittite carvings, to the supposed tomb of the ill-advised Tantalus. They were all very dull places to him. The foreigners did not know he was watching them, because he knew the country and all the roads, and had

71

high-powered German field-glasses. They would not know today that he was following them. He was well behind, far out of sight and earshot. He was not afraid of losing them. The road from the Sanatorium led only to Kara Göl: once on the road they could only go there, and then only return. There was a thin possibility that they might be meeting somebody who came over the mountains from the north. If so, the wrestler would watch the meeting through his binoculars.

The lake was girdled by pinewoods. They had the silence of pinewoods, the solemnity, the formality that comes from the absence of undergrowth. Şefik was quite right: it was inconceivable that anybody would have built a city in this inaccessible and infertile place. At the same time, a certain chilly eeriness made it easy to believe that a great crime had once been committed here: that a king had sought to hoodwink the gods by giving them his son, boiled, for dinner.

They had a picnic, better than Tantalus's, of cold stuffed vine-leaves and aubergines, and two bottles of Smyrna wine. Sandro had not brought any raki. Şefik was more tense than usual, but he did not get at all drunk, or say anything to Jenny about his future riches.

They started back after the siesta on which Sandro insisted.

Jenny again sat beside Sandro in the front, now able to see the other side of the road. As they left the belt of pinewoods round the lake, and started the bumpy descent towards the Sanatorium, Jenny was startled to see what, on the outward journey, Sandro's bulk had hidden from her. It was just visible from the car: a blaze of red beyond scrubby bushes, an area of several rough acres almost solid with poppies.

Jenny exclaimed; she pointed out the field of poppies to the others.

'Nature,' said Colly, 'used the old poster-paints a little

too liberally there, in my opinion. The effect is kind of vulgar, in my opinion.'

'Stop!' Jenny said to Sandro. 'Please,' she added.

Sandro shrugged and stopped the car. Jenny got out.

'They are weeds,' said Şefik. 'They are not interesting.'

'I like weeds,' said Jenny. 'It's flowers in gardens I can't be bothered with. This is really rather odd. Nothing else is growing here at all, just this fantastic carpet of poppies. Well, well. Nature's marvellous. What are you waiting for, you fat Wop? I want to go home and have my tea.'

'Ah,' said Mustafa Algan in the evening to the telephone in his shop. 'That is really naughty of Şefik Bozkurt. I wonder how he got hold of the seeds. No seeds were supposed to go anywhere near Izmir, no further west than Afyon. Little Şefik is not satisfied with the money I promised to pay him, he wants much more money. It is very bad security to have the crop growing so near a major port of loading. Some of the customs officials are not altogether fools. I am angry with Şefik Bozkurt. His behaviour is extremely dishonest. The crop must be destroyed. Şefik also. Presumably he is selling forward to the foreigners. They must be destroyed too.'

Chapter 5

Şefik's second sister Merih was helping her mother to bed. The father was already asleep, because he woke very early every morning, and lay wondering how he dared face another day. Only Şefik was still up and about in the sitting room of the villa. The women could hear him, through the gimcrack modern walls and floors of the house, moving across the room and settling down in a chair. He was perhaps reading: more likely mooning about the English harlot.

There was a crash and a tinkle of glass from the sitting room. Şefik shouted.

'What has he broken?' wailed his mother to Merih.

Şefik's shout turned into a scream. The scream ended horribly in a wet gargle.

His mother was by the window, and could see out into the street. She saw a very big man in dark clothes hurry away from the house; he moved quickly and quietly; within seconds he had disappeared round the next dark corner. Şefik's mother knew exactly who the man was, and what he had done, and why.

Merih screamed and fainted when she saw that her brother's head was almost severed from his body.

'You are completely positive about this?' asked the police inspector.

'Yes,' said Şefik's mother. 'He has been to this house many times, as our guest and the guest of our son. I know extremely well what he looks like. I know the back of his head as well as the front, and the way he moves. He does not look like any other man I ever saw.'

'Can you throw any light on the question of why he should do this to your son?'

'Yes. For days I have been afraid this would happen.'

'You *expected* it?'

'Yes. My son was many years younger than the Italian, much handsomer, more charming and intelligent. Naturally the English whore was attracted to him. Since she is the property of the Italian, he was violently jealous.'

'He said so?'

'It was in his face.'

It was no good talking to Şefik's father, who was in a state of hysterical collapse; but his sisters abundantly confirmed all that their mother said. They had all seen the frowns of furious jealousy on the Italian's face. They had all seen what caused the frowns – Şefik's attentions to the English slut, her shameless response to them, her evident preference for him. They had all been frightened of what the Italian might do to Şefik. Şefik had ignored their warnings; he had continued to pay obtrusive court to the bitch; only one result could be expected, and it had happened.

There was nothing surprising to the police in any of this. Turkish men own their women, and brook no challenge to their ownership. Revenge murder is the most frequent serious crime in Turkey, deriving either from long-standing feud or from sexual jealousy. Though the law must act, public opinion often exonerates. A man is morally entitled to kill to protect his own, or to pay back insult or injury: he is even morally obliged to. At the same time, families are not pleased to have a member in prison, however praiseworthy his crime, since they have to pay for his food.

The police were not surprised, but they were embarrassed. They were quite used to arresting foreigners: almost always layabouts on drug charges, occasionally smugglers of antiquities. They were *not* used to arresting distinguished European noblemen on charges of murder. But their duty was clear. They took sworn and signed statements from Şefik's womenfolk, and then set off for the Kizilçullu Palas Hotel.

Sandro allowed himself to be arrested, without fuss, at four in the morning. He knew that to resist, shout, show defiance, would make things more disagreeable for himself. The police had neat uniforms and pistols in holsters; they ran to ferocious moustaches. It was no discredit to their smartness that they badly needed shaves. They were quite polite; Sandro was equally polite. He knew the Turkish police were efficient and honest and very tough indeed; he knew they were concerned with the prevention and detection of crime far more than with human rights. He knew also that to these people an infidel foreigner, however rich or noble or physically powerful, was fundamentally inferior to a good Muslim of pure Anatolian ancestry. Kid gloves might not be worn.

Sandro was allowed to make contact with his consulate when it opened several hours later (the consul was an affable Maltese who represented a number of other countries besides Italy). He was allowed to see a lawyer found for him by the consul, and to talk briefly to his friends. He was not allowed to talk to his friends in private, or in any language unfamiliar to the police interpreter.

'This is unfortunate in one way,' said Mustafa Algan. 'Killing the Italian will now be quite difficult for you. Perhaps you had better not attempt it, unless you hear from me. At least he can do us very little harm. They will keep him in a cell for quite a long time before they have the trial. It is an ironic situation. Perhaps we should have expected it. Meanwhile the other two must of course be killed immediately. I cannot think why it

76

has not already been done. I expected you to report that they were dead when you telephoned this evening. It is very easy and safe for you. It will be assumed that a friend or cousin of Şefik Bozkurt has killed them, in revenge for his death. It amazes me that people do such things, but they do. It is convenient that we belong to a nation of savages with a sense of honour. Personally, I have never been interested in killing anyone except for a good financial reason. But then I am not a savage and I do not have a sense of honour.'

'This snarl-up is so screwy it's almost funny,' said Colly.

'Ha ha,' said Jenny bleakly.

'Seems the old bat has given the cops an absolutely positive ident. No doubt in her mind whatsoever.'

'There isn't. She'll be just as certain in the witness-box, if they have witness-boxes here. Unshakable. "Yes, that's the man I saw running away from my house two seconds after my son was killed." She'll have Sandro muttering threats for the last week, too. She'll probably remember seeing a bloody great knife in his pocket.'

'And believe every word she says.'

'Oh yes, and make herself believed. Trembling dignity and so on. True daughter of Islam.'

'High-class prosecution witness,' agreed Colly. 'Whereas I'll be lousy for the other side.'

'Can you actually give the old boy an alibi?'

'Just about. He was drinking Scotch in my room until around five after eleven. They'll assume he climbed out, so the night desk-clerk didn't see him. Had a car or maybe a scooter waiting around the corner. Roared up Kadife Kale, parked around the corner again, bust in through the window …'

'How is he supposed to have known Şefik would still be up? And alone?'

'He made a date with Şefik. Wanted a private meeting.'

'Then why did he bust in through the window?'

'Maybe to make it look like he wasn't expected – to make it look like a burglar or some kind of hooligan.'

'If that's going to be their case, it's as full of holes as your socks.'

'Yes, darling, but they don't have to fill the holes. They just have to put Şefik's mother in the box. The rest can be speculative as hell.'

'But he was with you till five past eleven.'

'Yeah. According to that creepy little lawyer, the cops were called from a neighbour's phone around twenty-five after, and got there at twenty-five of. It cuts pretty fine. Depends how long those women took to get to the telephone. My guess is, they'd shriek and fall around and say prayers for quite a while— '

'I hope you're not really as heartless as you sound.'

'No, darling, I am not. The point is goddam important. If they shrieked for ten minutes, then the murder was at a quarter after. That gives Sandro ten minutes to go to his room, dress in whatever they say he wore, climb out of the hotel, get up to the house, and cut off Şefik's head.'

'Impossible?'

'Sure it's impossible. Trouble is, they probably won't believe my evidence.'

'Why? You've got an honest face. Hideous, but honest.'

'Because I'm obviously lying to save Sandro. Because I'm in – what are those things people get in?'

'Jams?'

'Cahoots. I'm in cahoots with Sandro. We're old friends, partners in crime. Most of all, baby, I'm an infidel. My sworn oath isn't gonna impress them one little bit.'

'Hm. This is a bit worrying. Who really did it?'

'Another crook.'

'What do you mean, *another* crook?'

'*De mortuis* and all that, baby, but you have to admit last night makes Sandro's theory about Şefik look a lot more right.'

'Yes,' agreed Jenny sadly.

'Then the killer is either a crook he was with, or a crook he was against.'

'Against? A rival smuggler?'

'I guess so. Maybe a new group is trying to take over the local trade. Maybe Şefik belonged to a group that's trying to muscle in. That makes it a straight gangland job. Alternatively, his own crowd may have thought Şefik was double-crossing them. Maybe they were right. It's something that annoys criminals terribly. Heigh-ho, it's a goddam exhausting prospect, but we're gonna have to find out.'

'We are?'

'Of course we are. It's the only way to get Sandro off the hook. The old lady's gonna stand there, with her poor old arthritic hand on the Koran, swearing that Sandro trotted away from her home with a gory knife in his hand. Unless we can prove different, Sandro is cooked.'

'Do they cook people for murder here?'

'I don't know what they do. I don't want to find out. I don't want to think about it.'

'I wonder why last night?' said Jenny thoughtfully. 'Was there anything special about yesterday?'

'You mean, did something trigger this? Something Şefik did?'

'He came with us for a picnic.'

'But he didn't want to.'

'He didn't want us to go to the lake. But I can't think why. There can't be anything secret about the lake. Water, rocks, trees. He didn't try to stop us prowling round, once we got there ... Of course, it wasn't the lake he was worried about.'

'Right. It was something on the road to the lake. Some way beyond the hospital, but short of the lake.'

'Poppies,' said Jenny. 'That amazing patch of poppies.'

'Just weeds, like he said. And a little vulgar, like I said.'

'He was twice indiscreet about poppies. When he was a bit drunk, poor sweet, and he couldn't help showing off.'

'Yeah, but that didn't mean *poppies*. Surely it was just a way of talking about opium? A kind of euphemism, if I have the right word.'

'No good asking me about something like that. I know we thought hc mcant opium, but p'raps he actually meant poppies. Those poppies. Nothing to do with opium. He was going to make bead necklaces out of the seeds, or vegetable dye out of the petals, or ... something. Something quite innocent.'

'Then why not tell you about it?'

'It was secret. A new process. His new invention.'

'A secret from you? If he was trying to impress you, wouldn't he have given some kind of hint about something like that?'

'He did. He said "poppies".'

'And then denied he said it. Why should he do that, if it was something innocent, something creditable?'

'He might. Men are so odd. He was very mixed up, you know, he was really in a muddle.'

'A bad enough muddle to get himself killed.'

'The night after the day we all looked at those poppies.'

'Poppies, poppies, poppies,' said Colly. 'We keep coming back to that goddam field of useless, over-coloured weeds.'

'That's what we've got to do. Keep coming back to them. I mean, go and look at them again.'

'I had a horrible feeling you were gonna say that,' said Colly. 'And I have a horrible feeling you're right.'

'Is it done?' asked the little businessman from Istanbul.

'Yes. It was amusing, but at the same time very sad. Such a waste. I got some men to help me, workmen from the new road to Cigli. We took a barrel of gasoline and a power sprayer for insecticide. Here, written down, is an exact account of my expenses in the matter.'

'Did anyone see you?'

'Yes, of course. I said we were clearing a patch of waste land.'

'Which was true.'

'Certainly. We are instructed by the Koran to tell the truth at all times, and by Algan Bey to tell it whenever possible. What are the American and the girl doing?'

'They are taking the car again, the Opel from the garage.'

'Perhaps they will go somewhere quiet and empty, with no other persons near. This time I think you must come with me. We can kill them both at the same time, which is easier and more certain.'

'It is *not* what Algan Bey pays me for. But I am prepared to make an exception. Do you propose *just* to kill the girl?'

'No. She is very beautiful.'

'If she has been violently abused it will look more natural to the police.'

'Quite true. Besides, it will be a pleasant diversion for me, after so much hard work.'

'For us both.'

'Yes, why not? We will not kill them at the same time. We will kill him, then take hold of her. He will appear to have died trying to protect her, and she will appear to have died trying to protect herself.'

'It will be more than an appearance. It will be the truth. Both Allah and Algan Bey will be pleased.'

'And before they are found, you will be on your way back to Istanbul, and I shall be back at work in the warehouse.'

'Never having left it.'

'Never, as you say, having left it.'

The car jolted along the now-familiar road, up from the fat farmland skirting the Gulf of Smyrna, into the dry scrub and pinewoods on the slopes of Yamanlar Daği. Up here, poor farmers scratched a little wheat out of the

81

thin soil, and tended vines and windblown apple-trees. It was very clear and fine; the heat of the mid-day sun, which would have been fierce, was moderated by the blessed Imbat, the reliable west wind from the Aegean. Colly drove more slowly than Sandro would have driven, but after they had passed the Yamanlar Hospital the bumps in the road seemed just as severe.

'You know,' said Colly, 'it's possible that what happened last night had nothing to do with what happened yesterday.'

'Yes, of course,' said Jenny. 'The order to kill Şefik might have gone out a week ago, and the hit-man only got here last night. Or Şefik may have done something we don't know about, maybe in his office, maybe in Istanbul, which ended up ... like that. But actually I don't think so. Those poppies, after he talked about poppies ...'

'It's not a very large coincidence, baby.'

'No, but it's too large for me. I mean, for God's sake, that's why we're going there again, because the coincidence is too large.'

'Yeah. Today's botanical field-trip. Do you see the poppy? I see the poppy. Does the poppy tell you anything? The poppy does not tell me anything.'

'I admit it may not. But we must give it a chance to.'

'I already bought that, darling, repellent though the whole thing is. Was Şefik killed because he saw the poppies, or showed us the poppies?'

'I don't like the imp-something of either of those questions. Implications.'

'Me neither. If he's dead because he saw the poppies, what about us? We saw the goddam poppies. If he's dead because he showed us the poppies, what about us? We got showed the goddam things.'

'He didn't really look at the poppies at all. And he certainly didn't show them to us.'

'Anybody looking wouldn't know that.'

'Was anybody looking?'

82

'Who knows? If anybody was, what he saw was this car parked at the nearest point to the poppies, and you getting out to look at them. A guy watching from the woods might say, "Ah, I see it all. Şefik told them to stop the car just there, and told the doll to climb out and inspect his poppies." If that scene got Şefik killed ...'

'You know,' said Jenny, 'there's something to be said for being where Sandro is.'

'Yeah, but at least we're ready.'

'What for? Who for? When? Where? Why?'

'I guess we're not so ready,' admitted Colly.

Well behind again, the jeep followed the car to the Sanatorium and on towards Kara Göl.

'Ha,' said the man who looked like a wrestler, who was driving. 'This is very convenient. It is most helpful of them. It is an ideal place.'

'It shows,' said the Istanbul businessman, 'that Algan Bey was entirely right, as always. They would not have driven all the way up here, on successive days, to look at pine trees. Obviously Şefik Bozkurt was selling them his crop, in advance, exactly as Algan Bey said.'

'Why are they going to look at it again, having seen it?'

'They do not quite believe that red poppies can produce opium. They are taking some plants to be analysed in a laboratory.'

'I wonder,' said the wrestler, 'if they plan to come back and harvest the crop themselves?'

This made both men laugh very much.

'My God,' said Colly, 'somebody destroyed the evidence.'

Yesterday the rough ground had been a sea of scarlet. Now it was a desert of black. The job had been done thoroughly, with a considerable overkill. No trace of the poppies remained, and the frontiers of the bare, blackened earth extended, in uneven loops and bites, many yards beyond the edge of the area where the poppies had been growing. Wild poppies were visible here and there some way away; they were unmistakably of a different sort from those which Jenny had admired.

'Sprayed with gasoline,' said Colly, 'early this morning.'

'Soon after the murder. How do you know?'

'Has to be. The wind gets up mid-morning, most days. It did today. A fire this size would have whooshed way the hell across the hillside in a second, thataway, due east, into those trees. But they kept it local, burned only what they wanted. They'd wait till the sun was up, so a fast dry fire with pale flames wouldn't be terribly visible from a distance. But they'd make it as early as possible, so not too many people would be around.'

'There's nobody about now.'

'Why would there be, a useless, barren place like this, a road going nowhere? Anyway, nobody's gonna stand and stare, except us. Scorched earth is a terribly depressing sight.'

'We've made a bloody poor start,' said Jenny, 'helping Sandro.'

'Yeah. But it adds up. We lost the evidence, but we gained the moral certainty that Şefik was killed because of these ex-poppies.'

'I'd rather have the evidence,' said Jenny. 'I had the moral certainty before. Fancy going to the bluebottles and saying, "Somebody's been burning some weeds, so therefore obviously our friend is innocent." '

'We need a little more,' admitted Colly.

Sandro was having another conference with the local lawyer found for him by the Maltese who was his consul. Another and very senior lawyer had been retained by the Embassy in Ankara; this luminary was on his way to Smyrna, but the local man was being realistic rather than resentful when he deplored the wasteful extravagance of such a manoeuvre.

He said to Sandro, through an interpreter, in English, 'You do not deny, then, that you love the young lady.'

'Of course not, but I repeat that it is not the sort of love which— '

'Do you think the court will accept subtle distinctions between different sorts of love? Do you think it will accept that while ordinary love can lead to jealousy and to violence, a different sort of love – which appears no different – could never lead to any jealousy or to any violence? You do not deny that you have had a close relationship for many years with the young lady?'

'No.'

'Nor that you have often been quite alone with her, both in public and in private?'

'We are Europeans.'

'To stress that fact will *not* assist your case. Nor that you and she are in the habit of embracing warmly, of *kissing* with the *lips*, when reunited after a brief parting?'

'It is customary, among friends, in Europe— '

'Among friends in Turkey, also, but only friends of a certain type. I do solemnly assure you, for you to deny that you and the young lady have been lovers for a long time will be to invite the total incredulity of the court. As your lawyer, I must accept what you tell me, but *I* must tell *you*, off the record, that you invite my own total incredulity in this regard. Now – you do not deny that you felt displeasure at the friendship between Şefik Bozkurt and the young lady.'

'Displeasure is not right— '

'Why is it not right? You were seen to frown, to look at the deceased with a dark frowning face when he paid respects to the young lady.'

'It is probably true that I frowned.'

'Ah!'

'I liked that young man, and I was worried that he should make himself unhappy.'

'You met him two weeks ago, for the first time.'

'Yes.'

85

'Yet you were obsessed, eaten up, with worry about his heart, his tender feelings – while you were not at *all* worried about the feelings of the young lady, whom you had loved for years?'

'Her feelings were not a source of worry to me. They were not in doubt.'

'The Bozkurt family will certainly agree that her feelings were not in doubt.'

'The family see with a crooked eye. They are prejudiced, naturally.'

'A family which has just had a son murdered is entitled to a degree of prejudice, I think. It does not make their evidence untrue, nor, more relevantly, make it likely to be disbelieved by the court. Now – the Prosecution will have no difficulty in establishing that you have previously killed a man. That is correct?'

'Yes.'

'More than one man. Many men.'

'None out of jealousy.'

'You will be established as a man of violence, a man of guns and knives. I have to say that, from what you have told me yourself, this description seems to me a fair one, and will be accepted as such by the court. You must agree that it makes the possibility of violent action on your part far more likely on this unfortunate occasion. Let us be realistic, Count. I have never killed a man. I do not look capable of killing a man. No one who knows me would think it possible that I could have killed a man. I am small, thin, not strong, not young, living indoors, in offices, and courtrooms, engaged with books and clients and with pleading in the courts. It is inherently unlikely, evidence aside, that I would have committed a murder out of jealousy. Evidence aside, no court would fail to appreciate that. It would not be proof, but it would be very, very helpful to me if I were accused of such a crime.'

'I understand the point,' said Sandro.

'In addition, I do not possess a very beautiful yellow-haired English miss.'

86

'Nor do I.'

'The evidence will suggest otherwise. Now – you went to the house of death on numerous occasions as the guest of the Bozkurt family. You sat in a good light, I suppose, clearly visible from all angles. The mother of Şefik Bozkurt was present on all those occasions, and had the opportunity to examine you, in a good light, from all angles.'

'Yes.'

'You are, if I may say so, a most distinctive looking man.'

'Yes.'

'As to feature and as to build and as to movement. How many men have you seen in Izmir who look like you as to the face, are nearly two metres tall and a metre across, and move like a big cat? Those words may sound fanciful, but they are words that have been used. How many such men have you seen in Izmir? How many anywhere in the world?'

'A good cross-examination,' said Sandro patiently, 'would break down an identification which is understandable but a deplorable mistake.'

'A *good* cross-examination? A truly severe, harsh, bullying cross-examination of that old lady? She is severely crippled; she can hardly stand and cannot walk without the aid of a stick; she mourns the violent death of a beloved only son, which has quite unhinged her husband. Do you think the court will react favourably to the harsh cross-examination of such a witness? The more skilful and experienced the advocate, believe me, the less he would risk incurring the implacable hostility of the court by such an approach. It will be enough to lose the case, by itself.'

'Do you suggest,' said Sandro wearily, 'that I should pleady guilty?'

'Frankly, yes. There are mitigating circumstances which can be made to weigh quite heavily. The Turkish courts are, in this respect, perhaps more like the French than the British or American. The *crime passionel* is viewed with a comparatively indulgent eye, at least if committed by a man. It would, of course, be better if you were married to the young lady, far better, no doubt of that. But we must make the best use of what we have. It is not bad. I am quite sure my distinguished colleague from Ankara will give you the same advice.'

'I do not think, beyeffendi,' said the salesman in the carpet-shop in the Great Bazaar of Istanbul, 'there has been any more pilferage among the employees.'

'Good,' said Mustafa Algan. '*Nous avons encouragé les autres.* That storeman in Izmir, whose name escapes me— '

'Kemal.'

'—represents a sufficient discouragement.'

The storeman glanced at his master. He wanted to ask about the laboratory technician in Sille; he wanted to know how Algan Bey had seen, and how he had killed. There could be no doubt what had happened. Fikret saw the death, and Fikret was a man of the most perfect sanity and reliability. Superstitious dread of djinns or demons was no more part of his make-up than of the salesman's: but what were they all to think?

The episode had not been reported to Algan Bey, since he was always angered by hearing reports of matters which he already knew all about. He was too busy, he said, for his time to be wasted in such a way. If Algan Bey wanted to talk about the man in Sille, he would do so. If not, it would be injudicious of the salesman to mention it.

The salesman felt, as always, deeply privileged to work for so remarkable a man. He felt, as always, frightened of his uncanny master. His loyalty depended quite as much on the latter feeling as on the former.

Chapter 6

'We need a little more,' echoed Jenny.

She climbed onto an outcrop of rock at the edge of the burnt area. The herbs and plumy dry grass which had clung to it were reduced to blackened roots which crunched under her feet. There was a dead, charred smell from the black dust which her shoes stirred up: but the brisk wind from the sea had blown away most of the smell of burning, of gasoline vapour if there was any, and of anything the burning poppies might have smelled of.

From the top of her rock Jenny called, 'They've taken an awful lot of trouble, haven't they? They're probably still taking it. If they watched us yesterday, I should think they're watching us today.'

'You make a great target up there, darling,' Colly called back. 'Do you want to be a dead queen of the castle?'

Jenny was upwind of Colly, and did not hear him. She did not need to be told that she offered a good target to a man with a rifle. But the manner of Şefik's death made her sure, illogically, that their enemies would not fire rifles from a distance: if they had enemies, and whoever they were, and whatever their motives. Also, she did not think they would kill her without being sure, pretty soon afterwards, of killing Colly also: warned but unscathed, he could get away and cause them untold trouble. This must be as obvious to them as it was to her. Even if they had rifles, they would wait until they could get both in their sights. At the moment Colly was in good cover: no distant rifleman could get a shot at him. Jenny did not feel totally safe, but she felt nearly safe, which was good enough for her.

She looked slowly all round her.

Due east was the tree-smothered top of Yamanlar Daği, the mountain of Tantalus, hiding the taller summit of Manisa Daği, Mount Sipylus, the mountain of Niobe. South-east, fifteen miles away across the lush valley, rose Nif Daği, one of the nineteen mountains called Olympus. Due south was the lower bluff of Mount Pagus, the Kadife Kale or Velvet Castle of the Turks, as smothered in raw new buildings as Yamanlar by its pine trees and scrub. South-west, twenty miles away across the Gulf of Smyrna, rose the twin summits of the Two Brothers. They were all nice mountains: it was a nice view. The landscape was rugged but not awesome: it gave the sense not of wild remoteness, but of the continual impact of the sandalled feet of men over an enormous period. Legends lay on the ground as thick as the poppies that had been burned. Innumerable battles had been fought over the hillsides Jenny could see, and plenty of atrocities committed. It all looked very peaceful now, if she kept her eyes raised to the hilltops. But if she lowered them to the obscenely blackened and denuded ground, battles and atrocities seemed near and possible.

A flash came and went, like the single blink of a heliograph, on the track they had just travelled; Jenny saw it out of the corner of her eye; she thought it came from a mile away, between pine trees.

'Windscreen,' she called to Colly.

'Car moving or parked?'

'Moving. Why the hell didn't I bring some race-glasses?'

'Why the hell couldn't we bring Sandro?'

'Oh well,' said Jenny cheerfully, 'unless there's eight or ten of them I expect we'll manage. The great thing is to try and find something out from this.'

'You mean from them.'

'Yes. So let's kill them by degrees. I don't quite mean that. Especially as whoever's coming may not be them.'

'You mean, if they're perfectly innocent friendly strangers, we ought to kill them quick?'

'How do we know if they are,' asked Jenny, 'until they start cutting our heads off?'

Colly shrugged. 'I guess we have to wait 'til they start.'

'There they are,' said the man who looked like a wrestler.

He had stopped the jeep in cover, and stood up on the driving seat with his field-glasses.

'By Şefik's plantation?'

'Revising their plans to come and harvest it. The girl is looking this way, standing on a rock. I expect she saw the sun on this glass.'

'You should have lowered the glass.'

'Yes. You should have reminded me to do so. Do you think they expect us to come?'

'It is possible. They must know why Şefik was killed. They know we know about his plantation. They know we know about them. I wonder if they are setting an ambush?'

'For whom?'

'For us.'

'Who is us? We are two strangers in a jeep on the way to Kara Göl. I am a man interested in cutting down trees, you are a man interested in buying timber. What do we know about Sefik or poppies or foreign opium buyers?'

'You mean we drive up there, stop, talk to them in a friendly way?'

'Certainly.'

'They may suddenly shoot us, simply thinking it possible that we are what we are.'

'Although we might equally well be innocent persons passing by on the way to look at trees? No. You have been watching them for many days. Do you think they would shoot innocent strangers?'

91

'No,' admitted the little businessman.

'Come along, then.'

The jeep bumped round the corner into sight, having advertised its approach up the hill, for a long way, by the roaring of its engine and the rattle of its bodywork.

Colly's hired Opel, its hood raised, effectively blocked the track. He stood in apparent preoccupation, staring down into the Opel. His gun was out of its holster and in the side pocket of his cotton jacket. He had not expected to need a gun on this Turkish holiday, but habit had made him bring it; since Sandro's arrest it had never been more than inches from his hand.

Jenny was out of sight of the jeep, crouched behind the rock on which she had stood. She had not brought a gun to Turkey, but now had Sandro's, which the police had not found when they searched Sandro's room.

Rattling and roaring, the jeep stopped three yards from the Opel.

Jenny, crouched behind her rock, could not see the jeep without being seen. She would take her cue from what Colly did and said. She watched him look up and grin ruefully.

He said, in careful Turkish, 'Do you know anything about cars? This one has stopped, but I do not know why.'

The driver of the jeep grunted. He climbed out of the jeep and approached the front of the Opel. He was a very big, powerful man. He moved like an athlete, gracefully. In his bulk and his graceful movement there was something reminiscent of Sandro.

The thought blazed into Colly's mind: he *was* like Sandro. Hurrying along a dark street, seen only from behind, he might be taken for Sandro. He had been taken for Sandro, by Şefik Bozkurt's mother. This was Şefik's murderer.

He was no use to them dead. They were no use to Sandro dead. It was a tricky position.

Colly backed away from the open front of the car, still ruefully, inviting the big man to look at the engine.

The big man did not at once lean over the engine to peer into it. He looked all round, slowly. He did not see Jenny, who was hidden by her rock and flat on the ground. The way Colly had disabled the car would baffle any but a very expert mechanic.

'You are alone?' the big man asked Colly.

If they had been watching the Opel, following it, they knew Colly was not alone.

'At this moment, yes.' said Colly. 'A friend is with me. My friend has gone for a walk. I do not know where, or how far.'

The big man nodded. He was in no hurry to help Colly with the Opel. He was in no hurry to continue his own journey up the track.

There was another man in the jeep, a small man in a neat dark suit who looked like a businessman from a big city. His face was dimly familiar to Colly, but held no message for him. He had, perhaps, seen him in the streets of Smyrna, or in a coffee-shop or a bar. Maybe the man had been tailing them. If so, he did it brilliantly. Colly had not been aware of a tail, and there were very few people in the world who could tail him without his knowing about it. He only suspected the tail now because of the slight familiarity of the man's face. This was interesting and worrying. It suggested they were up against professionals of the highest class.

The small, respectable man got out of the jeep. On little pointed black shoes he began to climb the bank beside the track. One hand was in a pocket of his neat dark jacket. It might be holding a gun. It might be holding a cigarette or a piece of chewing-gum. There was no reason he should see Jenny, Colly thought, unless he climbed to the top of the rock. But he might easily do that, to see if Colly's companion was anywhere near.

Colly thought it likely that either the big man or the little businessman spoke English. Perhaps both. One or other might speak any European language both Colly and Jenny knew. They would not know Swahili or Urdu. It was inconceivable that they should ever have heard a word of either.

Colly appeared to address the big man, who still stood placidly beside the front of the Opel. He said to him, smiling, in Urdu, 'This big man looks like our big friend. Therefore I think he is the one who killed the young man.'

The big man frowned for a moment. But his face cleared immediately. Probably he realised that Colly had been speaking not to him but to an invisible ally nearby. Maybe Colly's cleverness was not very clever after all.

They obviously knew Colly's companion was a girl. They would think that made it easier for them. Turks would never expect a girl to carry a gun, and be expert in its use. Such a thing would be entirely outside their experience, shocking, unthinkable.

Another aspect was that they wouldn't attack Colly until they had located Jenny. He was as safe by the car as she had been on her rock, for the same reason. She might be a witness to a killing, and get clear away. Against that, there was nothing to stop them finding her within seconds. The moment they found her the bomb could go up. If there was a bomb.

There might be no bomb. It had to be borne in mind that these people could be perfectly innocent passers by. The big man was a big man who moved gracefully, and could be taken, by an hysterical old woman, in the dark, from behind, as Sandro. That was all Colly knew about him. The other man had a slightly familiar face. There could be a million reasons for that. If he lived in Smyrna, the familiarity of his face was not even a coincidence. There was nothing peculiar about the behaviour of either of them, except that they seemed to be in so little hurry. Well, maybe they *were* in no hurry. They were ahead of their time, for an innocent

94

rendezvous up at Kara Göl. They were glad to kill a few minutes. It happened to everybody.

Colly wondered if they ought to have played it differently – gone on up the track in the car, as soon as they knew somebody was coming after them. Hidden in the pinewoods, let these people come and look around and go away again. Then what? They'd be jumped another time, if these were killers. And they'd learn nothing. They'd give no help to Sandro. Awkward as this situation was, it was the right choice to have made.

The big man at last looked down into the guts of the car, and started fiddling with the plug-leads and distributor. He took his eyes off Colly. He could do so safely. The little dark-suited businessman was standing on the roadside bank with Colly full in his view. He kept an eye all round, too, waiting for Colly's companion to return. He had still not spotted Jenny, who could hardly be ten feet from him. Or maybe she was more. Maybe she'd crawled away, as she could, using cover that nobody would think was cover, and she was well hidden some way off, watching and waiting. No, thought Colly, she'd stay close, she'd never risk losing contact, she'd never lose sight of him in case he was attacked, or get out of range of his voice.

It would all be so easy if they *knew* these people were enemies. There were a dozen well-tried manoeuvres. For example, Colly could suddenly have a fit – scream, roll on the ground, foam at the mouth. That would infallibly distract both men for the necessary half second. Jenny would come up behind the small man, slug him, and get a drop on the big man. No problem. But if the men were innocent passers by, simply stopping to help, extending traditional Turkish hospitality to luckless foreign wayfarers? Then such an attack would make Sandro's situation much worse. His friends would have shown themselves people who made violent, unprovoked attacks on well-meaning strangers. It would fit all too well with the scenario the law already had, with the prosecution's picture of a blood-thirsty man with bloodthirsty friends.

The situation seemed to have frozen, as though photographed. It was almost as quiet as a photograph. The big man leaned over the front of the Opel, but his posture suggested that he was waiting for something rather than doing anything. The small man stood at the top of the bank, alert, looking round over the burned poppy field, and up and down the track, and looking at Colly. Colly stood with his hands in his pockets, eight feet from the car, slouching apathetically, his expression patient and rueful and weakly amiable, his senses as alert as an animal's. The sun blazed down on the dry, herby uplands, but the wind still blew fresh from the sea. A lizard scuttled among stones. The breeze blew puffs of powdery ash from the burned acres of the poppy field. It was very peaceful.

Jenny lay wondering what to do. She was the joker, the catalyst. As long as she lay hidden Colly ought to be safe, because they could not risk killing one when the other was out of their sight. She was uncomfortably aware that she was not well hidden, curled like a snake at the foot of the rock on which she had stood. If the small man climbed the rock he would see her. Jenny had glimpsed his feet as he climbed the bank. He had on little, flimsy, pointed shoes, big-city shoes. If he started climbing rocks they would be shredded. Vanity, or meanness, or concern for the comfort of his feet would, perhaps, keep him off the sharp and abrasive sides of the big rock. If so, Jenny could stay where she was as long as she liked. How long did she want to stay there? It was safe but it was not helpful.

Jenny managed to catch fleeting glimpses of the big man by the car, after Colly's message in Urdu. She saw what Colly meant. It was morally certain that this big, graceful brute was the man Şefik's mother had seen in the dark street. Why was it? There were plenty of big

96

men in Turkey, and some who looked like weight-lifters and moved like dancers. Why this one? Because he was here. Almost nobody came here, far beyond the Sanitorium; it was on the way to nowhere, except a deserted lake in the pinewoods. This was arid, useless ground. This big man's being here made him the right big man. It was a moral certainty, but it was not enough of a certainty to tighten the finger on the trigger of Sandro's gun. These people had to declare themselves, declare war. They would do so – they *might* do so – when Jenny appeared. Till then the situation was petrified. They were all turned to stone by the eye of one of the mythical monsters of this place, a Gorgon or a basilisk. When Jenny moved they'd all come to life. The thing to do was to plan how best to move.

What was needed? To force an aggressive response from them, if they were enemies, to make them show their hands. But to do so in a way that would seem innocent if they weren't enemies. That meant keeping the gun hidden. To be, at the end of the move, in a good position for battle, if there was going to be a battle. That meant having the gun ready.

The gun was a problem. Jenny was wearing a cotton shirt over a skimpy bra, cotton jeans over bikini-size stretch pants, and rope-soled canvas shoes. That was all. She had left a sweater and a headscarf in the car. She carried cigarettes, lighter, a scrap of handkerchief. The handkerchief was too small to conceal the gun in her hand. If she put the gun inside her shirt, or in the waistband of her pants under the shirt, she might not be able to get it out in time, if time turned out to be vital. And in Jenny's experience it always did.

Making all her movements as small as possible, as slow as possible, Jenny unbuttoned her shirt and wriggled out of it. She felt the hot sun on her shoulders and the rough ground on her ribs. She was aware that her bra, skimpy and transparent, was far from decent. That was the least of her worries. What her shirt now did was hide the gun: it could hide her bosom again when this was over.

Jenny thought out her next movements, the probable reaction to them by the Turks, Colly's and her own reaction to that reaction, and the likely outcome. Her decision taken, there was no point in delaying. She took a deep breath and went into her act.

Colly heard a dry, droning cry from the top of the bank, from under Jenny's rock. Jenny shot to her feet, rigid, trembling, screaming. Colly had seen this one before: otherwise he could not have realised this was not a genuine epileptic fit. He was surprised for a fraction of a second to see that Jenny was practically topless, until he realised that her shirt was hiding her gun. Moaning, Jenny pitched forward. She doubled up and rolled down the bank to the track. She fetched up between Colly and the car. She lay, rigid and twitching, on her back on the ground. Her eyes were open but only the whites were visible. There were flecks of foam on her lips and chin.

Colly stood as though stupefied, his mouth hanging open. He glanced, his face aghast, at the big man by the car and the small man on the bank. He saw that they glanced at each other. The big man made a small gesture with his chin. The small man skittered down the steep bank in his natty little black shoes. He knelt beside Jenny on the track. At the same moment the big man, with a movement so swift that it was like a single jump, was close beside Colly and behind his shoulder. It was as though he wanted to comfort and reassure Colly, while his friend ministered to the poor young lady. It was natural that, since he had been mending a car, he should be carrying a heavy wrench.

They were good. Quick reactions and convincing performances. They were in position for the kill, without losing their innocence. They might guess Jenny's fit was assumed. They wouldn't guess about her gun.

The big man's face, close to Colly's, was serious,

concerned. He held the wrench loosely in the hand further from Colly. If he moved his arm as quickly as he moved his legs, he could smash Colly's skull before Colly knew it. Then Jenny would be raped before she too was murdered.

The small man, kneeling beside Jenny, looked the picture of kindness and anxiety. He cooed comfortingly. He put a hand behind Jenny's head, lifting it a little off the ground. Colly saw that Jenny's bra was exceptionally scanty and transparent. The deep pink of her nipples was clearly visible through the lacy stuff, which covered little else of her beautiful firm breasts.

The Turks were given to rape. They loved it. Their invasion of Cyprus was notorious for the soldiers' repeated and violent rape of Greek Cypriot women of all ages, old women and very young girls. It was natural male behaviour, earning no moral condemnation.

The small man still seemed sympathetic and gentle. He glanced at his friend and at Colly.

Colly knew what was going to happen. The small man was going to make some gross assault on Jenny. Colly was to lunge forward, outraged. The big man was to smash his head with the wrench.

It happened. The small man suddenly took hold of Jenny's bra, with his free hand, at the narrow point between the cups. He pulled violently. The flimsy garment broke and came away from her chest, baring her breasts. Colly lunged. He went not towards Jenny but into the big man, knocking him momentarily off balance because this was the last thing he expected Colly to do. The big man swung the wrench. But he was off balance and Colly had already danced out of his reach. The big man came after Colly, the wrench high. Colly screamed with simulated terror. The big man laughed. It was enough. Certainty was established. Colly shot the man in the shoulder, with the gun still held out of sight in the side pocket of his jacket – the gun he had never let go of.

The smaller man had somehow got a knife in his hand. He must have had it in his sleeve. It was very quick and neat, the way he had flicked it out of his sleeve into his hand. More proof. Only professional killers could do tricks like that with knives. The small man had the point of the knife at Jenny's throat. He barked something at Colly. Colly did not understand the words but the meaning was unmistakable. Colly was to surrender or the point of the knife would go into Jenny's throat. Probably not far. He would still want to rape her before he killed her.

Jenny's right arm was at her waist, wrapped in the cotton shirt. She twisted her wrist and shot the small man. The bullet went in below the chin and out of the back of the skull. The round was quite heavy, a .38, and the man was knocked momentarily backwards and sideways before he fell forwards on top of Jenny. She wriggled clear and stood up, unwrapping the shirt from the gun. There was blood on her bosom.

'Sorry,' she said. 'That wasn't the shot I meant.'

'You didn't have a whole lot of choice, baby,' murmured Colly. 'You did fine. Now cover yourself up, will you, before I start feeling like a Turk myself.'

'What a prude you are.'

Jenny wiped the blood off herself with a handful of coarse herbs. She put on her shirt. There were new holes in it, from the bullet which had gone through half a dozen folds.

The big man was kneeling on the ground. He was holding his injured shoulder. He had dropped the wrench. Suddenly his uninjured arm whipped across his body from his shoulder to his jacket pocket. Colly stepped forward and kicked his wrist before the gun was out of the pocket. Jenny came round behind him, buttoning her shirt. She took the gun out of his pocket. He made a movement to stop her, to grab it, but Colly gestured with his own gun inches from the man's face.

'Now,' said Colly carefully in Turkish, 'you will answer some questions.'

The big man, crouched on the dusty track, must have been in great pain from the bullet in his shoulder. He did not show it. He did not show any fright. His face was wooden. If it had any expression, it was a look of anger, of impatience.

Colly said, 'Who do you work for?'

The big man spat at him.

Colly tried, for an hour, in the broiling vertical sun. He promised various kinds of violence, torture. He fired bullets into the ground, inches from the man's legs. He threatened him with the dead man's wicked knife. He got nothing. The big man called him a pig, a foreigner, an infidel. He called Jenny a whore. That was all he said. He was unmoved by any threat. The only way he showed he had been wounded was by fainting after an hour.

'Maybe the cops will have better luck,' said Colly.

'Oh,' said Jenny. 'Ah. Is that the plan now?'

'This guy's a self-declared hoodlum. So's his friend with the big knife.'

'Who says he is?'

'Circumstances say so.'

'Described by us and who else?'

'Well, for Chrissakes … Oh. Hum. Yeah, I see what you mean. The dialogue might be a little sticky.'

'Your car broke down,' said Jenny, trying to sound like a Turkish police officer, 'These gentlemen on their way to Kara Göl stopped to help, as all good Turks are bound to. The one you didn't kill testifies they were going to the lake to look at the trees, or swim, or something. The British female had a fit. One of the kind gentlemen loosened her clothing, which is the right first aid when a British female has a fit. The other kind gentleman held a wrench, on account of he was kindly trying to mend your car. He happened to raise the wrench, to swat a fly or scratch his head or wave to his chum. You shot him. Absolutely unprovoked. The female shot the other kind man who was trying to help her.'

'What about the knife?' said Colly.

'What knife? The surviving gentleman testifies that he never saw it before. It's not the dead gentleman's knife, it's your knife, which you often kill people with. Whose fingerprints are all over it?'

'Well, they had guns.'

'In the first place, who says they had guns? It's a wicked libel against the dead as well as the living. They're your guns. People like you naturally have an arsenal in the car wherever you go, in case you decide to kill somebody and then tell lies about it. In the second place, half the adult males in Turkey carry a weapon of some kind, to protect themselves and the honour of their women. Yes,' said Jenny in her policeman's voice, 'you two are exactly the friends we'd expect of this Italian murderer. The way you've been acting confirms our conviction of his guilt. You'd better go to gaol too, the female for the unprovoked murder of a respectable Turkish citizen, and the American hippy for grievous bodily harm on another respectable Turkish citizen.'

'That's a horribly convincing scene you wrote,' said Colly glumly. 'Why in hell won't this big slob tell us anything?'

'For one thing he's got a lot of guts,' said Jenny. 'For another, he doesn't want to convict himself of murdering Şefik. For a third, he's more frightened of his boss than he is of us.'

'Then we haven't achieved a goddam thing,' said Colly.

'Yes we have,' said Jenny. 'We've got ourselves in much worse trouble than we were before.'

Chapter 7

'Being a law-abiding guy with old-fashioned ideas,' said Colly, 'my instinct at a moment like this is to hightail it to the cops. But you convinced me that's a pretty bad idea. So what *do* we do with your friend and mine?'

'Burn mine up in the jeep,' said Jenny.

'Check. And big brother?'

'Killing him is no good, is it?'

'Not a lot, not if we want to get Sandro off the hook, which I suppose is still the general idea.'

'We ought to keep him with us. And keep asking him questions.'

'Sure, but I don't think we'll do that. For one thing, he won't answer. For another, a confession under duress, which he denies the moment he feels safe, is not gonna help us any. Third, I don't think I know this country well enough to snatch one of its citizens and keep him incommunicado for a few weeks.'

'Then we either take him to the cops or let him go.'

'God damn it, we have to let him go. Goes against the grain, but we have to.'

'What does he do?'

'Stays away from the cops, I hope. Reports back to his boss. Maybe we could watch him do that? I wish we could tail him, but I'm afraid we can't, since he's a pro on his own ground … Then he or somebody else has another try at killing us, I guess. Maybe we can fix for some cops to be watching, that time.'

'Well,' said Jenny dubiously, 'Maybe. I wish I knew

why they were trying to kill us. Why they killed Şefik. What's so special about these bloody red weeds. We know they're not opium. They're the wrong colour. So what are they? ... You know who's behind all this?'

'Well, no, baby, I don't think I do. Do you?'

'No. But I think it's Sandro's pal. Mustafa Thingummy.'

'Why?'

'Why not? He's the only Turkish criminal I've ever heard of, if he is a criminal. We met Şefik in his shop. Şefik wasn't there to buy carpets, because he couldn't possibly have afforded any of those carpets.'

'Şefik was gonna get rich growing poppies.'

'Yes, poor lamb. And after he showed us these poppies, without meaning to, he got rubbed. And we nearly did, because we saw them. And Mustafa Thing has a lot of peculiar lolly in Zurich.'

'Okay,' said Colly. 'I'm convinced. Half-way convinced. Well, it'll still do as a hypothesis. But where does it get us? We already hijacked and searched one of his trucks. We looked at his store and we looked at him. Even Sandro gave up at that point. What more can we do?'

'I don't know,' said Jenny. 'But I expect Sandro would like us to think of something.'

'There is that. In his place I'd feel the same.'

Colly searched the body of the little neat businessman, and the unconscious person of the big man. There was nothing significant on either. They had not expected anything on such obvious professionals.

They put the body of the little man in the jeep. They drove the jeep and the repaired Opel up the track to a place where one car could pass another. They drove the jeep on a little. Colly smashed it scientifically against some rocks, then tipped it over a steep bank. The dead body was considerably bashed about, which would hide the fact that he had been shot through the head. They set fire to the jeep with the body in it.

They turned the Opel and drove back to the burned poppy field. The big man had disappeared. He had come to: he was either hiding or on his way back to Smyrna. Or maybe friends had come after him and picked him up. Colly drove with his gun in his lap, in case they turned a corner and met those friends.

They would know the big man again, if he crossed their paths, as soon as he would know them. Maybe sooner, if they did something about their appearances.

'Yes,' said Jenny. 'Phoney passports. Some dye. Contact lenses. Then we'll go to …'

'Where?'

'I don't know. I'm getting an idea. I'm not chasing it, I'm letting it chase me.'

'Then go slow, baby, so it catches you quick.'

Jenny led Colly to a carpet store. She chatted about carpets and carpet selling to the owner of the store. She mentioned, in the most natural way, the wonderful display of carpets she had seen in the store of Mustafa Algan in the Great Bazaar in Istanbul. The Smyrna storekeeper knew Algan Bey, was very proud to be able to claim the acquaintance of so eminent a man. Algan Bey had been in Smyrna for ten days earlier in the year. He had honoured this store with a visit. He had not been altogether contemptuous of some of the carpets on offer. It was remarkable that so elderly a gentleman could still travel as much as he did, going everywhere in search of fine carpets to buy. No doubt he was less frail than he looked.

'Did he come to buy carpets?' asked Jenny innocently.

Assuredly not. No carpets were made in or near Smyrna. The town was an important port, and the centre of a very rich farming area, but it had no tradition of carpet-making. Algan Bey had come here on vacation, perhaps, as many wise people did, or to see friends, or …

The movements and motives of a tycoon like Algan

Bey were beyond the speculation of a humble provincial member of his profession.

'I want to know,' said Jenny to Sandro in the gaol, 'where your carpet-selling friend has been travelling.'

The police interpreter listened gravely, and took shorthand notes.

Sandro said, 'To very many places where carpets are made.'

'Yes, and other places. Such as here. For ten days. This spring. On his hols, or something.'

'He is well known,' said Sandro thoughtfully. 'His movements are not secret. If he stays in a place, people will notice and remember. I will give you a name and a telephone number in Istanbul.'

They got enmeshed in Sandro's Istanbul contacts. People referred them to other people. They were hours on the telephone, on several successive days.

At long last they established that during the previous year Mustafa Algan had been to Kayseri, Smyrna, Bursa, Konya, Sivas and Antalya. The carpets of Kayseri, in Cappadocia, had once been fine but were now mass-produced and beneath the contempt of a serious dealer. To Smyrna he had also come for reasons unconnected with carpets. Bursa in the north was still a source of some of the very finest carpets; likewise Konya in the south-central highlands, and Sivas far in the east. No carpets were made at Antalya, on the south coast, or anywhere near it. From Sivas it was believed that Mustafa Algan Bey had made a journey much further east, but it was impossible to confirm this without indiscretion.

'There,' said Jenny. 'That gives us a sense of direction.'

'Does it, darling?' asked Colly.

'No, not really. But I shall go mad if we don't pretend it does. Long shots are better than no shots. This may

106

not be such a wild outsider, actually. He went to Bursa, Konya and Sivas about carpets. At least, I s'pose we can safely assume he did. Why did he come here? If Sandro's right, he came here to fix up an opium or heroin smuggling operation, this being a perfect place. Maybe he was employing Şefik. I don't like to agree about that, but it does answer some of the questions. Anyway, that's a feasible reason for him to come here, which carpets aren't. He went to Kayseri and Antalya. Not for carpets. Why?'

'Do opium poppies grow in those places?'

'I don't know.'

'Or red ones, like Şefik's, of unknown purpose?'

'I don't know. Let's go and look.'

'The cops won't like that.'

'The cops won't know it's us. Let's make some passports.'

Mustafa Algan made a gentle exclamation of extreme surprise to the telephone. 'The *girl* shot him?'

'Dead. While pretending to have a fit. Having stripped herself half naked. The man shot me. Then they tried to question me. I did not tell them anything.'

'I am sure you did not. Well, well, it is all intensely surprising. I wonder if ... Could the boy's voice have been a young woman's voice? The young woman I saw? Such a pretty little thing, and young enough to be my granddaughter. It was she and her friends who searched my truck, and left my carpets lying all over the road? It is scarcely credible. It is most immodest and unfeminine behaviour. Also it is irritating. I am beginning to feel persecuted. All I ask is to be left alone. Well, well, we are forewarned. I hope you are in the hands of a good and trustworthy doctor. You will be paid the usual bonus for personal injury. It will, of course, become a regular pension payment if by any chance you do not recover the full use of your arm or shoulder. Let us pray to Allah that your cure is speedy and complete, not only for your sake but for mine too. The fact that I pay pensions does

107

not make me enjoy doing so. I also do not enjoy the continued attentions of these accursed foreigners. I feel quite bigoted on the subject, which is unusual for a man of my tolerance.'

After Mustafa Algan had put down the telephone, his salesman said hesitantly, 'Those particular foreigners are indeed accursed, beyeffendi, but it is on foreigners that our operations depend.'

'True. But you will have observed that under no circumstances do I consent to any contact with our customers. In this shop, in regard to carpets, yes. In the other transactions, no, never, never once. I do not know who our ultimate purchasers are. I do not want to know. They do not know who I am. I continue insistent that they shall not know. This is not wholly a matter of security. It is also a moral position, about which I feel strongly. I deplore drug addiction. I am revolted at the thought of those degraded addicts in such places as London. I want to hear nothing about them, or their suppliers. I refuse to know anything about them. You may see a certain dishonesty in this position?'

'No, indeed, beyeffendi.'

'Oh? You should. I detected it myself, until I realised that I was comparable to a gunmaker or a wine-grower or a horse-breeder. By making a gun I am not responsible for a murder. I am an honest technician meeting a legitimate commercial need. M. le baron de Rothschild is not responsible for drunkenness, nor an Irish horse-breeder for a death in the hunting field. I produce and export high quality chemicals. That is all I do. What people do with them is not my responsibility, or of any interest to me. I certainly have no wish to meet the fat European criminals who buy my products and degrade the youth of their own countries. Disgusting! I should probably be quite rude to them.'

News of Sandro's arrest reached the European newspapers. It was given large coverage in Italy, small in

108

other countries. Jenny's and Colly's names were kept out of the news, since they were neither arrested nor held as material witnesses.

A leading Italian criminal lawyer, a friend of Sandro's, went to Smyrna. He had long conferences with Sandro, and with the local Turkish lawyer found by the consul and the more eminent one found by the Embassy. The Italian studied the evidence and the procedure of Turkish criminal justice. He was extremely depressed. He believed Sandro's story, but he did not think any Turk would believe it. Neither of the Turkish lawyers believed it, although Sandro was paying them.

A coded cable to the Tucker Trust office in Milan resulted within twenty-four hours in the chartering of a motor-yacht, called the *Uccello Bianco*, in Palermo. On board were skipper, engineer, deck-hand and steward. The skipper, Giorgio Mazella, was looked at askance by both police and customs, but he had never actually been caught. He had a reputation for fine seamanship and total discretion.

The *Uccello Bianco* was chartered on behalf of a M. and Mlle Marais. But they did not come to Palermo to join the yacht. They were to be picked up in a certain way, at a certain place, in the Gulf of Smyrna, at or any time after a certain moment. The captain's orders were confidential, exact and bizarre.

Another coded cable, to another Tucker Trust office, produced a bank account in Istanbul, with plenty of funds at the disposal of M. Marais, and cashing facilities in a number of towns in various parts of Turkey.

Letters arrived at the *postes restantes* in these and other towns, addressed to M. Marais and Mlle Monique Marais, from an office in Geneva and other places in Switzerland.

A flat package, sent express, arrived for Colly Tucker at

his hotel. The postmark said that it came from Berne. Colly unwrapped it in the foyer of the hotel, under the eyes of a dozen people. He held up, with a rueful face, a copy of a recent archaeological guide to the Aegean Coast of Turkey. Locked in his room, however, he did shameful things to his nice new book with a razor-blade. The binding had seemed, on close examination, a little bulky. This was because the binding contained two Swiss passports.

A third coded cable went to the Tucker Trust office in London. Its assistant manager, with the decoded message in his hand, telephoned the Earl of Teffont in Wiltshire. He said, guardedly, that his lordship should not take too literally reports he would shortly be getting about his daughter's disappearance. It might appear that Lady Jennifer and her American companion had been drowned. The appearance would be misleading, and reports of their death exaggerated.

'Damn,' said Lord Teffont. 'The miserable child's doing it again. Obliging us to go into mourning or into hiding. I don't know which I dislike more.'

'I suppose they're trying to help poor Sandro,' said Lady Teffont.

'Yes. I wish there was some way we could help him, too.'

'Colly will do everything he can.'

'I know. I wish I could believe it'd be enough. From what I heard at the Italian Embassy, Colly has got to produce a miracle.'

Ahmet Muammar was delighted to hire his boat, for the day, to the silly American. It was not a very good boat. The American said he was competent to handle the Ford engine and, if he found himself running before the wind, the little red sail. Ahmet was glad to spend the day relaxing at home with his grandchildren, although when he saw the American's woman

110

he was sorry not to be going with them on their outing.

They came to the port from the prison, where (as all Izmir knew) their friend the large Italian was awaiting his certain conviction for murder. The girl (as all Izmir knew) was the cause of the murder. It was no surprise at all. Ahmet Muammar would have murdered anybody for her, in the days of his hot youth.

They brought with them bathing things, an extensive picnic in a basket, books, binoculars, cameras, and other baggage. It seemed to Ahmet a heavy and complicated burden for a day's trip up the gulf. He himself would have taken only a few oranges and a bottle of wine, but he had seen enough of foreigners to know that they did everything oddly.

Ahmet went aboard with them, and started the engine while they stowed their baggage under the half deck. He scrambled onto the quay and untied the fore and aft mooring ropes. He noticed with surprise that the girl coiled them neatly, a thing he had never dreamed of doing. The American puttered out of the harbour, threading between ships.

The Imbat, the wind from the sea, was blowing briskly. The boat bounced away cheerfully over the bright waves. The girl, whose hair was the colour of sunshine, turned to wave at Ahmet, who waved gallantly back. He even came near to removing his cap.

The boat was pointed due west, the shadow of its mast on the waves before it, towards the promontory of Kara Burun thirty miles away at the mouth of the Gulf of Smyrna.

'There she is,' said Colly.

He looked with distaste at the seventy-foot white motor yacht; he liked being propelled over the water by wind, not diesel-oil.

Ten minutes later they went up the side of the *Uccello Bianco* on a beautifully varnished ladder. Their miscellaneous baggage followed them aboard. The captain said he had been waiting at the rendezvous for three days; he had wondered if there was a change of plan, but the radio telephone told him to go on waiting.

Colly and Jenny went below immediately to change. Neat new clothes, in neat new suitcases, were waiting for them in their cabins. Colly blessed the efficiency of his family company's Italian staff, but Jenny was not enthusiastic about her new garments.

They put their discarded clothes, the empty picnic basket, and other oddments into Ahmet's boat. They set the boat adrift. The west wind would take it back to Smyrna in time.

Colly and Jenny were well accustomed to changes of identity. With what they had with them, what they had borrowed, and what they had innocently bought at a drugstore, they had the means.

Since Sandro was Italian, Jenny English and Colly American, they had decided to avoid all these nationalities. Neither spoke perfect German. They elected to be French Swiss, from Geneva, a city they knew.

Jenny dropped a few years. She became a gauche, convent-educated girl of seventeen. Her shoulders were rounded, her posture awkward, her movements clumsy. She turned in her toes, and had a tendency to bump into doorposts and small tables. Her complexion was greasy and yellowish; there were spots on her chin. Her hair was a drab mousey-brown, dragged back into a pony-tail.

Colly added a few years. He became the brisk, brash executive of an international tobacco company, taking his daughter on holiday after her graduation from the convent. His hair was greying, and cut *en brosse*. He wore assertive horn-rimmed spectacles. His teeth were brilliantly white. His handshake was crushing. His movements and gestures had a suggestion of military precision. He looked a man who did his exercises night and morning, took vitamin pills, and expected to be Managing Director.

The difference in appearance was not so tremendous in either. But there was in both a huge difference in manner, in evident personality. All the things anyone would remember about Jenny were swamped in the shy dinginess, the overpowering dullness, of little Monique Marais. All the self-effacing, shambling, rueful gentleness of Colly was swamped by the mid-Atlantic energy of Etienne Marais.

No one, seeing them together, could doubt their relationship – the twitch of rebellion under the dutiful diffidence of the daughter, the spasm of irritation in the protective concern of the father.

The captain and crew of the *Uccello Bianco* obediently erased from their minds all recollection of a golden-haired English girl and a brown-haired American. They had never seen such persons. They had also never seen a scruffy half-decked motor-boat with an illegible name and a smelly engine.

The yacht motored at twelve knots north-west to clear the promontory, then turned south towards Samos.

Ahmet Muammar's boat was recovered and restored to him. He wailed that it was damaged, hideously scratched, practically stove in, but to other eyes than his it looked exactly the same as before.

The girl's clothes were seized by Ahmet's daughter Zezahat. To her chagrin, however, they were useless to her, as she was fond of pastries and sweet things. The man's clothes were useless to anybody. Few beggars would have consented to wear them.

An extended search by customs launches and army helicopters was eventually abandoned. Theories ran up and down the streets of Smyrna like the little boys selling shoelaces and whistles. The foreigners had eaten and drunk heavily, swum too soon from the boat after doing so, and thus got cramp and drowned. The girl, overcome by remorse at her responsibility for the death of Şefik Bozkurt, had drowned herself, and the man had perished in an attempt to save her. The man had made lecherous advances at the girl, who was of course the property of the imprisoned Italian; incensed by her rejection, he had drowned her, and then, either contrite or frightened, had drowned himself.

The Italian seemed less affected by the news than might have been expected. He was, no doubt, absorbed in contemplating his own predicament. It was ironic that the whore for whom he had committed murder was now herself dead. The result of his case was not likely to be influenced one way or the other by the absence of his friends. Their evidence in his defence was not going to be believed, when set against the evidence of Şefik Bozkurt's mother.

The news broke in London and in New York. Jenny was much mourned. Messages of condolence poured to her parents' Wiltshire house. The butler said that the Earl and Countess were away, which was true, and that he was unable to get in touch with them, which was a lie.

A few people who knew Jenny and Colly well were sceptical about their deaths. But, because they knew them well, they kept quiet about their doubts.

There was no particular hurry. It was still a long time before Sandro's case would be heard. But neither Jenny nor Colly was in a mood for leisurely cruising. The yacht made good time threading between the coast and the string of Greek islands, passing Kalymos and Cos and Rhodes, then turning east, passing the bay of Marmaris and the grim coast of Lycia, then turning north into the gulf of Antalya, with the spectacular profile of Mount Climax to the west and the high peaks of the Taurus, snowcapped, rising beyond the Pamphilian foothills.

Colly studied the coast through binoculars.

'I dunno,' he grumbled. 'Maybe it means something.

114

There's certainly a raft of them. Seems like there's practically fields of them. I guess it's natural, but it certainly doesn't look natural.'

'What are you talking about, fool?' asked Jenny.

'Poppies.'

Chapter 8

Wendy Duxbury felt a despairing pessimism new to her. Normally she was an optimist. A sort of optimism was necessary in her job, for keeping the belief that it was worth while, for keeping sane. As an experienced social worker in a rough part of Manchester, she had seen horrors enough over the years – Irish families so feckless that their swarming children had no hope, none, of growing into responsible members of society; Jamaican landlords viciously extorting, evicting, blackmailing their own people; Indian children bought and sold for miserable dowries; the old dying of cold and the young of back-street violence; the valiant and pitiful efforts of herself and her colleagues hamstrung by the cutbacks in local government spending, by indifference and callousness and hostility.

All that was old stuff. So was addiction. There were pushers of all colours, lots of them, driving big purple cars and buying furs for their women: and their underlings were creeping everywhere in the discos and clubs and pubs. They started the kids on very small fixes, often sold at a loss. Once they were hooked the quantities went up and so did the price. The young junkies had to turn to theft, mugging, prostitution in order to pay the steeply-hiked prices of the pushers. Old stuff.

But there was something new, something horrifying and inexplicable. Wendy Duxbury was as sickened and appalled as when she first went into social work, as a little idealist straight from college in 1950. The first case she actually saw was a middle-aged black musician, a bongo drummer, who tried to kill himself with a piece of splintered wood before dying of failure of the central nervous system. This demented effort at suicide was something a far-gone addict might do if he failed to get his fix. But the man had just had one. The empty syringe was on the floor, and the autopsy proved what the hypo suggested. It was perplexing as well as disgusting.

Other cases followed. The very worst, to Wendy Duxbury, was a young girl who worked as a hostess in a club. She had locked herself in the club's staff washroom for her fix, having just got the stuff from her regular source, a customer, unidentified. Once locked in, she must have made a lot of noise, but it wasn't heard over the club's amplified band. At least nobody admitted having heard anything. She had smashed up the bowl and the cistern with a strength far beyond her strength. It could only have been her, alone in the little reeking cubicle, because of the locked door. Some time later somebody saw the blood seeping out under the door. She was badly injured by the damage she herself had done, but that had not killed her.

In the observation of Wendy's department, a kind of dreadful pattern began to emerge. A minority of addicts only were affected. There seemed no discernible difference between them and others. Registered addicts, who got legally imported and legally processed heroin from reputable chemists, were in no case affected. Some of those whom the new horror struck attempted suicide. This caused Wendy to guess that they suffered some sudden, overwhelming agony, either of mind or of body. This remained the oddest thing, as a fix brings peace; it ends the horrors: it dissolves pain. Few of the suicides were successful. These few involved high windows or oncoming trains. Most of the suicides failed. This was because the people were too confused or distraught, were

117

blinded or directionless or demented: or it was because they died before they killed themselves.

It was difficult to put together many facts. The pathologists had broken bodies to work with; at best their subjects were far gone in degeneration from the human to the half-starved, half-sane, broken zombie. None of the social workers, or any of the police, saw one of these moments of apparent devil-possession, nor managed to get an eye-witness account. Addicts are secretive. They lock themselves in lavatories, or hide in deserted basements. And they are inhabitants of a shadowy, tight-lipped world, where people come and go and die, and use false names and nobody asks questions or makes friendships or cares or dares to get involved with anybody.

A small meeting at the Home Office in London turned to the most disquieting item on its agenda.

The information came from most parts of the country. There was far more information from some places than from others; it was suggested that this represented variations in the strength of local social services, and the extent to which they had succeeded in infiltrating their local drug scene, and in the alertness of police officers and police surgeons, rather than in the actual incidence of the phenomenon.

The phenomenon was the sudden and fairly horrible death of 476 heroin addicts. It most cases it was established, in others assumed, that death followed rapidly on intravenous injection. Cause of death was usually diagnosed as brain damage, of a kind associated with addiction but far more dramatic, in the cases where autopsies had been required. A sort of berserk violence was often associated with the moments of death, as though the victims had brief periods of wild insanity before oblivion.

'It must be a shipment of impure heroin,' said an official. 'In some way the stuff's become contaminated

118

with some kind of nerve poison. An alkaloid from a plant harvested by mistake with the poppies? It must be something like that. Possibly only one shipment is involved, a packing-case full brought in by one man. Possibly the supply is now exhausted or nearing exhaustion.'

'Possibly,' said a colleague, 'there have been a series of shipments of this terrible muck. Possibly there are to be many more.'

'Yes. That is so.'

'Is it possible, might it be possible, either on medical or pathological evidence, or by analysis of samples seized, to identify the impurity? To pinpoint the source?'

'No, sir, not as things stand. As far as doctors are concerned, these symptoms are outside any medical experience we are aware of. Addicts may be extremely violent, almost insensate with desperation, in their efforts to get money to buy a supply of their drug. But once they've got it they're peaceful to a fault.'

'They just squat in a corner.'

'Yes. No form of morphine or diacetyl morphine known to us has the effects described in this hair-raising material. There is clearly something very wrong with this stuff, something poisonous and murderous, but the doctors can't tell us what it is.'

'Nor the pathologists?'

'No. Samples have been taken from a variety of these – casualties. But what the pathologists have found is heroin, or evidence of recently injected heroin, or conditions compatible with addiction to heroin.'

'And we haven't secured any of this stuff before it's been taken?'

'Not as far as we know. A certain amount has been seized, in the usual places – cross-channel car ferries, airports, yachts, merchant seamen's baggage – and an average amount in the possession of pushers. Samples have been analysed. What we have is heroin. Either there's something funny about some of it that we haven't detected, or we don't happen to have got hold of any of the funny stuff.'

'We must keep trying.'

'Yes, sir.'

'And praying, I suppose.'

'That, too.'

There was what should have been a breakthrough.

Wendy Duxbury in Manchester got to know a family called Wilkins. Eric Wilkins was a small newsagent and tobacconist in a back street near Salford Station. He and his wife were worried stiff about their daughter Karen, who had got into a bad set. There was a boyfriend, who called himself Thunderbolt, they particularly feared. When they talked to Karen about it, she screamed that she trusted and needed Thunderbolt. Wendy talked to Karen. She saw immediately what the parents were too naïve to see. The kid was on the hard stuff. Wendy laboured with her, but Karen was rebellious, and anyway she was hooked.

Karen died. Everything about her death followed the horrible pattern of the rest. Her parents were heart-broken. They identified Thunderbolt to the police. Thunderbolt was taken in. He was Shane Stubbs, from Oldham, with a background of Borstal and a two-year suspended sentence for making an affray hanging over him. Shane was an addict, too, so it was easy to get him to talk. He got his fixes cheap and regular in return for a bit of pushing. He had sold Karen the last and fatal tablets. They came from a man called the Ashtray.

The Ashtray was a flabby, yellow-faced hospital porter with this profitable sideline. He was far too frightened of his employers to sing, though he was shown both stick and carrot. But patient and meticulous detective work established a link between the greasy porter and the Italian manager of a snack-bar. This character had disappeared. But a neighbour, snooping through net curtains, had seen the irregular visits of a big red Vauxhall car. The driver of the car wore a camel-hair coat. He always went in, and came out again with a packet of sandwiches. But he was in there longer than it took to buy a packet of sandwiches.

The snoopy old woman had the number of the car.

The car belonged to a small garment factory in the city, which employed non-union immigrant female labour at starvation rates. It was used by four or five different people, all of whom looked as though they wore camel-hair coats. The one identified by the snack-shop's neighbour was called Clarence Morris, forty-nine, who had a very nice suburban house, a secretary much prettier than his wife, and a lot of money in the bank.

The secretary was called Sandra Pornick. She admitted that her flat was beyond a secretary's salary. Mr Morris was ever so kind, a very generous gentleman.

Clarence Morris's salary, director's fees and commission totalled about £15,000 a year. He was spending much more than that, what with Sandra and foreign holidays and his children at private schools. He explained it affably. He was a close student of greyhounds, and made the extra money at the dog-track. He had all the betting-vouchers to prove it; he kept them for his tax-accountants.

His betting was astonishingly successful – outsiders backed as though they were already home. He always went to the same bookmaker, Mo Smith, whose accounts were in some confusion. He admitted losing a lot to Clarence Morris. But many of the bets had been hedged, with the offices or the Tote, and he had some steady losing clients too.

Mo Smith had thousands of contacts, ranging from the impregnably respectable to the undoubtedly criminal. He could not be criticised, let alone charged, for laying a bet to a villain. As he said himself, he couldn't refuse a bet from a man who'd once stolen a car – he'd lose his licence. Some of his clients lost as regularly and

121

heavily as Clarence Morris won. The bets were probably phoney. Clarence Morris was written down in Mo Smith's book as having had a large bet on an outsider, after the race had been run; and a man who was paying Clarence had a large losing bet. Mo was simply a post-office, taking a commission on the way. He even paid the betting-tax on Clarence's 'winnings'. It was impossible to prove anything, especially as the losing bettors insisted that they *had* betted and lost the money.

Mo's losing clients were investigated. But they probably knew they were going to be looked at, because Mo probably told them. Probably they were buyers of whatever Clarence Morris was selling, but they had time to hide what they'd bought, put on innocent faces, and warn their own other contacts to stay clear. Some were professional criminals. All of them stank. But there was no law against losing a couple of grand at the dogs.

At this stage of the investigation Clarence Morris fell under a lorry in Mosley Street. The driver was cleared of all responsibility. It seemed that Clarence was pushed, but he might have been pushed accidentally. No one saw the pusher. Clarence's own employer or supplier decided that the heat was on Clarence. He closed down the operation in the most final way. The trail ended; the hunt ran out of scent. No doubt a new pipeline would immediately open, with new greedy hirelings who would last as long as the big man thought they were useful.

By this time a further 162 heroin addicts had died terrifying deaths, in their lonely squalor, immediately after injecting themselves.

'The people supplying this stuff,' said a man at another meeting at the Home Office, 'must know about its effects.'

'Yes, by now. I don't suppose it worries them. They're killing people fast instead of slowly.'

'And losing customers.'

'Not so very many.'

'*What*?'

'An appalling number, of course, but not compared to the sum of addicts. This awful stuff is a very small proportion of the total amount of heroin being distributed.'

'And,' said another glumly, 'if we can't identify it, it's not to be supposed that the pushers can. What are they to do – each destroy hundreds of thousands of pounds worth of heroin, *in case* their stock includes a bit of the funny stuff? Losing a few customers is nothing compared to the scale of that write-off.'

'So as long as it's still coming in, people are going to buy it and die from it.'

'Yes.'

People were buying it and dying from it all over Europe.

To the Home Office came confidential reports from officials in France, Holland and Sweden. In these countries had been noted, as a new and recent phenomenon, the inexplicable deaths of drug-addicts under peculiarly dreadful circumstances.

The worst case was that of a group of eleven Dutch students, naïvely experimenting, who all died in evident torment within a few minutes of giving themselves their first-ever injections.

In none of the four countries was any heroin seized which, on analysis, explained what was happening. It was all outside the experience, in all the countries, of doctors, pathologists, social workers, police, or other drug addicts.

There was, as there always had been, a strenuous and sustained effort in all the countries to fight the drug traffic. No more could be done than was being done.

Wendy Duxbury's despair was echoed in many grim international meetings.

'Where does it come from?' people asked.

The answer could include large areas of the earth's

land surface – south-east Asia, China, India and Pakistan, Afghanistan, Turkey, many countries in Latin America.

On balance, Turkey was the most likely. The bulk of the opium, morphine and heroin imported into Western Europe was probably grown in Turkey. Having a substantial legal opium-poppy crop made it easier for Turks to grow it illegally.

The Turkish government was concerned and co-operative. Wherever the familiar white opium poppies grew, samples were taken for analysis. Resin and raw opium were sent to the laboratories of the complaining nations for their analysis, too. Derivatives were injected into guinea-pigs.

The stuff was perfectly all right. All of it was perfectly all right.

But just as many deaths continued to be reported. And the deaths were just as horrible.

'The government scientists,' said Mustafa Algan, 'are making a great fuss about the quality and purity of Turkish opium and its derivatives. I know this from a source in Ankara. It is a very expensive source, but the information I buy is sometimes almost worth the money it costs me. Not this time, however. This information is utterly irrelevant to us. To other producers, perhaps legal ones, but not to us. If there is one thing my conscience is *quite* clear about, it is the quality and purity of my product. It is a source of pride with me. I would no more sell an adulterated product than a fraudulent carpet. It is agreeable to have a clear conscience. It is an aid to digestion. I recommend it.'

Jenny took the binoculars from Colly, and stared at the rocky coast below Mount Climax.

Here and there the cliffs formed themselves into natural terraces almost inaccessible except to goats or helicopters, high above the sea. These terraces blazed with splashes of lurid colour – with dense drifts of pink and vermilion poppies.

'See what I mean?' murmured Colly. 'And we know Mustafa Algan was in these parts. Accepting your crazy hypothesis ...'

'Yes. What do we do?'

'I guess we go and look at those poppies. I can't imagine they'll tell us anything, but looking at poppies seems to be what starts the action in this business.'

'Yes.' said Jenny. 'We look at the poppies, and we see if they seem to be the same sort as my poor little Şefik's poppies.'

'His looked like weeds.'

'No, not quite. More like some awful garden.'

'I'll buy that. At least, I'll go along with it in the absence of anything else. I guess Şefik's were bigger than the other poppies up there, the ones which were definitely weeds.'

'How do we know the others were definitely weeds?'

'Because they didn't get burned.'

'Oh yes. All right, clever.'

'I wish I was more of a botanist,' grumbled Colly. 'I wished we'd picked some of Şefik's poppies when we had the chance. I wish Sandro was here. I'm out of my depth, frankly. I want my hand held. Anyway, I guess what we do, is we pick a few of those poppies, if they look like Şefik's, and send them off in this tub, and have them analysed.'

'That's going to take a long time.'

'I know it. It's one of the six million things that's bothering me.'

'What is the analyst supposed to be looking for?'

'If Sandro's right, opium. But opium poppies are white. Nobody ever heard of a commercially grown opium poppy any other colour but white. At least, I don't think so.'

'Then p'raps,' said Jenny, 'it's a completely different drug. Or not a drug at all. As I said weeks ago, it's nothing to do with drugs. It's something like a ... dye? A new sort of birdseed? Glue? Petals for throwing at weddings?'

'Yeah. But confetti and that other stuff doesn't fit with Şefik's head being cut off. Or with that party we had on the road to Kara Göl ... Anyway, we'll do some sight-seeing, and you can pick some flowers in a girlish kind of way, and then we'll see where we've got to.'

They explored Antalya, in the role of prosperous, serious Swiss tourists.

They crossed the town in horse-drawn four-wheeled cabs, each pulled by two tough Anatolian ponies; the cabs were brilliantly red (as red as Şefik's poppies), with highly polished brasswork; they frightened pedestrians and goats out of the way with honking bulb-horns or a jangle of bells. Jenny and Colly dutifully inspected the three-arched Gate of Hadrian and the odd pink minaret of a vanished mosque. They saw a few other tourists and a multitude of street hawkers, who tried to sell them flutes, razor-blades, balloons, cucumbers, and lottery tickets.

Jenny wanted to buy a bunch of the high-bobbing, high-coloured balloons, and let them go over the sea one by one. But she thought this would be out of character with Monique Marais.

The shops of Antalya were not large or smart. There was nothing in this remote provincial capital to compare with the internationalised luxury of Smyrna, or the tourist traps of Istanbul. But in the picturesque muddle of the Old Town, half way up the steep hill above the harbour, they found a carpet seller.

It was possible to mention, as casually as in Smyrna, the wonderful carpets sold by Mustafa Algan in the Great Bazaar in Istanbul. The response was the same. The distinguished Algan Bey had honoured Antalya with a visit in the early spring. He had drunk a cup of coffee in this very shop, with the proprietor. He was not, perhaps, very deeply impressed with the carpets on sale here, though sometimes it was possible to find good ones two hundred kilometres to the north-west, over the big mountains, in Konya. Why was he here? Ah, but to marvel at the ancient temples on the coast. He went by car eastwards to Perge and Aspendos, as did all visitors. He went by boat down the coast to Finike, no doubt, to Demre and to Kaş. Those were much harder places to get to, much less often visited. But Algan Bey said, in this very shop, that he wanted to see them all before he died.

They came out into the steep little alley, where the gables of the houses almost met over the street.

Jenny wrinkled her nose and sniffed. The air was full of the smell of fresh-baked bread, of kebabs slowly roasting over charcoal, and of resinous wood-smoke from the stove of a nut seller. The smell of the streets of Antalya was very much nicer than that of Istanbul.

Colly said, 'Those places Mustafa Algan went to by sea – you know where they are?'

'No,' said Jenny, still sniffing wistfully.

'They're in, or under, those cliffs we passed.'

'Where the vulgar poppies are growing.'

'That's right. I guess there *are* ruins in or near all of those places. Every goddam neighbourhood in this country seems to be lousy with bits of temples and stone guys who lost their noses. That gave Mustafa Algan a perfectly good excuse to go that way. It gives us one, too.'

'But we must go the other way as well,' said Jenny. 'East, by car.'

'Yeah. Anybody would, anybody innocent, any tourist. They're better known places, and easier to get to. I agree we have to plod along that way and look at amphitheatres, horrible as the prospect is, just to look normal.'

'And in case there are poppies there.'

'That too, baby.'

They joined a party in a dolmuş, a large taxi holding as many passengers as the driver could collect who were going in compatible directions. They came ashore from the *Uccello Bianco* in the morning, and strolled to the main square of the New Town where big, battered American cars waited for trade. They heard a cry, '*Perge'ye*,' – to Perge, which was the nearest of the archaeological sites along the coast to the east.

The rest of the passengers in their dolmuş were a party of solemn cultured Germans, under the control, if not the command, of a grim woman in a paramilitary uniform, like a scout-mistress. The camouflage of M. and Mlle. Marais, already good, became perfect.

They trundled through orchards and olive-groves, past a small new airport on the coast, and by big fields of cotton and then bigger fields of grain. Wherever there was rough, uncultivated ground or stony outcrops among the flat fields, poppies grew, brilliant red, sometimes densely packed.

They turned inland, climbed for a short distance, and came to a deserted Roman town set rather sadly, Jenny thought, in the middle of nothing.

There were poppies everywhere.

They marched briskly among the ruins, suffered if not welcomed by the Germans as part of the audience of the scout-mistress's lectures. Jenny picked a small bunch of the wild scarlet poppies, which wilted immediately in her hand. To clutch a handful of dead flowers somehow fitted the character of Monique Marais, at once drab and a little fey.

'I swear these are just weeds,' she murmured to Colly. 'They're exactly like the ones you see everywhere. They're not like Şefik's.'

'I think you're right. All the same, we'll have them analysed, as a control. If these are normal, innocent

128

poppies, and some of the others show up different, then that difference is what we're looking for.'

They went on (dragooned by the Germans) to Aspendos and its almost perfect Roman theatre, and then to Side, once a bustling port, now a jumble of fallen marble beside a tiny modern village.

By the time they squeezed back into the dolmuş, Jenny had had more than enough of ruins. She had picked a few poppies at each stopping place, and was careful to keep the bunches separate. The Germans thought it rather *gemütlich* that the shy little Swiss girl should cradle bunches of wilted poppies on her lap, in the crowded car, all the way back to Antalya.

Colly tried to telephone, from an hotel, to Istanbul. He wanted to have arrangements made for a laboratory to analyse the poppies they had and the poppies they were going to get.

But telephoning from Antalya was not at all like telephoning from Smyrna. From that busy international seaport, Colly had been able to get through to Istanbul numbers with little delay, by paying at a special 'no waiting' rate, four times the normal rate. But these facilities was unheard of in Antalya. There was no demand for it, none foreseeable. At the normal rate, Colly learned, he had no hope of getting through to Istanbul that day. The following evening was hopefully suggested as the earliest possibility. The urgent rate, three times more expensive, involved a delay of some hours.

'There's a lot to like about this country,' Colly said, 'but ...'

As far as urgent communication went, they had put themselves out of touch.

'Goddam,' said Colly. 'It's something I just didn't expect. I should have done a hell of a lot more homework.'

'You didn't know you were going to need it,' said Jenny. 'Usually you hate making calls in a big hurry.'

'Yeah. Usually I say, the whole of the rest of my family are always making calls in a big hurry, and that makes enough Tuckers making calls in a big hurry.'

'Anyway, usually you've got Sandro holding your little hand.'

'Also true. Well, we do have the yacht's radio-telephone.'

'But not to anybody in Istanbul.'

'Not to anybody in Istanbul, and not to anybody who doesn't have a Tucker Company code book. I'd hate to have a lot of nasty-minded strangers listening in while we blow our own cover, and say exactly where we are, and fix for a bunch of poppies to be analysed because they look like Şefik Bozkurt's poppies.'

'I wonder where they are,' said Mustafa Algan musingly, in his shop in the Great Bazaar.

'At the bottom of the Gulf of Izmir, beyeffendi.'

'It is possible. One cannot deny the outside possibility. But one of the things I have discovered about the American – indeed, almost the only thing generally known about him – is that he is, or was, an expert and very experienced yachtsman. He has sailed all over the world, in boats of all kinds and sizes, in quite dangerous waters. There was not a high wind, or a storm of dangerous waves, or a treacherous, unexpected current, on the day they disappeared. And where are the bodies? Why not washed ashore, in a gulf almost totally land-girt and with a prevailing wind from the sea? I wonder what they look like.'

'We know what they look like.'

'We know what they used to look like. Well, they still have significant attributes in common with personalities that we know. They are a man and a girl, foreign, enquiring into my affairs. At least, I must suppose that is what they will be doing. Fortunately, I have friends all over Turkey. Absolutely everywhere, as you know. That is because I am generous and honourable in all my dealings. All my friends, everywhere, are to be invited in the most courteous way to watch out for a man and a girl, foreigners, enquiring into my operations, or behaving in any other clearly dubious fashion. Whoever finds and correctly identifies them will earn my undying gratitude and goodwill. More even that that, perhaps. Certainly anyone who correctly reports their dead bodies to me will earn much more than my gratitude.'

'Everybody will be told, beyeffendi, everywhere. It is fortunate that we are not obliged to rely on the telephone.'

Chapter 9

Turkey was shocked by three completely inexplicable double murders. The victims were all foreigners. They were all robbed, but to such paltry effect that robbery was not, in any of the cases, a convincing motive for murder. It was not the work of a single homicidal maniac, or crazy xenophobe, because great distances of bad road separated the three episodes, which were, however, almost simultaneous.

In each outrage, a man and a woman, together, were killed. In all other respects, the cases were as different as they could be.

A young American couple on honeymoon, John and Marcia Franks, went on a day trip to Ephesus with a large party in a bus. They left their party during the afternoon to stroll up the Bulbul Dağ to look at the ancient wall of Lysimachus. They were a little overwhelmed by the earnest culture of the group; they still exulted in each other's company, and wanted to be alone together. John was twenty-eight and looked younger. Marcia was twenty-three and looked older; she was a thin, leggy blonde girl, whose skin had been coarsened by the sun of her native California, and whose hair had undergone too many changes of colour.

They climbed a few hundred feet, hand in hand, going slowly in the hot sun. Three men, local shepherds or labourers, watched them incuriously, squatting in the shade of the masonry of the wall on the hillside.

John took a picture of Marcia, posing her against a

general view of Ephesus below them. He was slugged from behind at the same time as Marcia was grabbed. Both were garotted with pieces of flexible electric wire. John's camera was stolen.

A Swedish mother and son were exploring the Byzantine church of St Sophia, just outside the city walls of Trebizond, nearly seven hundred miles from Ephesus as the crow flies, and part of an utterly different world.

The Swedish lady was a prim teacher of mathematics, recently retired and also recently widowed. She looked exactly what she was, with grey hair tied in a knot behind, gold-rimmed spectacles, and sensible clothes. Her son was a doctor of thirty-five, gayer than his mother but not much. They were greatly impressed with the newly uncovered frescoes in the church, and shocked that during the war the ancient building had been used as a store for drums of gasoline, which had ruined the marble floor.

They walked from the church down a grassy slope to the edge of the Black Sea. They looked with distaste at sand like soot, at a great flotilla of floating melon rinds nuzzling the edge of the land, and at four ferocious looking but indolent men with rough clothes and big moustaches.

Mother and son were followed back towards the city walls by the four men. They thought nothing of it, because they saw nothing of it. There was a moment when they disappeared from sight from the church, and from the sight of the peasant women who shuffled, with big, black, needless umbrellas, along the beach.

They were both clubbed to death, with large stones which were found beside their bodies. The old lady's spectacles were taken but the lenses must have been in smithereens, unless they were removed before her head was smashed in.

In Ankara, almost exactly midway between Ephesus and Trebizond, a rich middle-aged Brazilian and his French girl-friend left a cocktail party given for, and by, people they did not know. Both were celebrities, in the world of the gossip columns if not in that of actual achievement. This explained their invitation to the party. Both lived at parties and for parties, having nothing else to do, which explained their acceptance of the invitation.

The girl, whose passport misleadingly described her as an actress, had been bored at the party, and bored during her two days in the ugly, uninteresting concrete city of office-blocks and apartment-blocks. She was not quite a beautiful girl, but she was generally found very attractive. Her protector had curly grey hair and a mixed reputation. He led the girl, holding her possessively by the arm above the elbow, towards his Mercedes, which was parked between street-lamps.

They got into the car in the middle of a bitter and pointless little quarrel. No doubt this distracted them. They never saw the two men in the back seat. They were killed almost simultaneously, almost instantaneously, each with a long and very sharp knife just below the jawbone.

'I suppose,' said Mustafa Algan, 'it is better to try too hard than not hard enough. And it is certainly gratifying that my request has been so speedily acted upon, in such remote places. But perhaps, without giving offence, we can suggest a *little* more care? I understand that the Swedish woman in Trebizond was small and fat and seventy years old, and the American female many centimetres taller than our little English acquaintance. The confusion is scarcely justifiable. On the other hand, I must in honesty admit that I do not really mind how many Europeans are killed, unless they are on their way to this shop for the purpose of purchasing carpets. I do not mind, as long as I am not expected to reward all these irrelevant deaths. Certainly, it is far better, in such situations, to err on the side of safety. In any case of authentic doubt, let us by all means play safe. Let our friends, by all means kill anyone who truly might be the ones we are looking for. English law, you know, whimsically lays down that it is better that a thousand guilty persons should escape than that one innocent man should be executed. I take a precisely opposite view. The law of Mustafa Algan lays down that it is *much* better that a thousand innocent persons should be executed than that one guilty one should escape. Two guilty ones, in this case. I merely ask, in the interests of simple humanity, that our friends do not kill, in a general way, too many people who could not possibly be the ones we are concerned with.'

'They tell me,' said Colly to Jenny, 'that we can easily land from the yacht, in a lot of places, for maybe the first fifteen miles of the coast— '

'The other coast? The one we've looked at from the sea?'

'That's the one. There's a broad coastal strip, like the one on the side we explored, growing cotton and citrus fruit and stuff. Then what they call the Bey Mountains come right up to the coast, as we saw, and for the next forty or fifty miles there's only a few places where we can land. So they tell me.'

'I expect they underrate us.'

'I guess they do, baby. But remember about staying in character, not doing too many obviously weird things, not drawing too much attention to ourselves. Landing from the yacht at the foot of those cliffs is gonna seem very weird. And then, from what we saw, there's often a hell of a climb up a lot of nasty looking cliffs before we get to where the poppies grow. Don't forget we have to keep doing it. It's no good grabbing just one bunch of poppies from one place. We have to have a selection. At least, I guess we do, to make any sense of this. If we keep doing all that – keep landing in screwy places, and climbing dangerous cliffs, just to pick a few flowers, people are sure as hell gonna notice. Having noticed, they're gonna talk. Somebody's gonna listen. And after a while, we might as well not bother with dyed hair and phoney passports.'

'All true, darling,' said Jenny. 'Very, very boring, and very badly put, but true. We'll have to do our landing and climbing at night.'

'Oh no. Oh no. We may not be much use to Sandro as we are, on current form, but we'll be even less use with broken legs and busted arms and smashed skulls and fractured— '

'Stop it. I get the point. Okay. So what?'

'So we get to the poppies by land.'

'From here?'

'Sure.'

'But we can't. There's no coast road, you said, until Finike, if that's what the first place is called, and that's fifty miles away. That's what you said. I expect it was a lie or a stupid mistake, but that's what you said.'

'Yeah. Since then I discussed sightseeing with the Vali— '

'What valley? Or do you mean valet? Whose valet?'

'The provincial governor. Also the tourist office. What we do is what everybody does. We go behind the mountains. We come down on the coast the far side of the goddam mountains. Then we can get along the coast easily one way, as far as we want, not so easily the other way, and maybe not as far as we want, *but* behaving reasonably. Looking normal. We can peek at all the poppies we want, and pick all we want, and stroll back to the town for tea.'

'Why tea? Can't I even have a drink?'

'You're a woman,' said Colly austerely. 'In these parts you're no better than a chattel.'

'Oh yes. What town is it I'm strolling back to for my raki?'

'The ones we passed on the yacht. The ones Mustafa Algan apparently went to see. Finike, Demre, Kaş.'

'Poppyland.'

136

'We thought so.'

'But we can get to those places on the yacht. We can land at them. They're ports.'

'Yes and no. Demre isn't. It was, but not any more. Something shifted. And what we have to see, from what they tell me, is the gorge of a river that runs into the sea at Finike, and a place up beyond the head of that gorge.'

'Why?'

'Because somebody just happened to mention, just happened to let fall in the way of conversation, that those are amazing places for poppies.'

'All right. We'll look at poppies, and I suppose we'll get ourselves killed, like all those couples they keep talking about on the radio news.'

'Yeah. We want to be a little more careful who we turn our backs on.'

Colly tried to find out if there was an adequate anchorage for the *Uccello Bianco* at Finike. Half Antalya had clear ideas on the subject, but the ideas differed. Some said there was a deep cove protected by a massive breakwater, where a fleet could ride safely during a hurricane. Others depicted a bare shingle, or sharp rocks, exposed to every wind and wave. Colly assumed the truth was about midway between these extremes: Finike must be a natural shelter, since it was one of the ancient Lycian fishing and trading ports; but not a very good one, or more people would know about it, as they knew about Marmaris and Smyrna. There was no chart that helped – or, if there was, it was not in the chart-case of the *Uccello Bianco*, or purchasable in Antalya. Colly's map was noncommittal; no better map was to be bought locally.

Colly ordered the skipper of the *Uccello Bianco* to go to Finike and tie up there if he could; if not, to anchor as near the shore as he could; and to watch out for them. If Finike seemed a really dangerous lee shore and a southerly gale threatened, the skipper was to go to Kaş, about thirty miles further west: and failing that, to stand out to sea until it was safe to come in and wait around at Finike.

'Look out for us – let's see – any time from midday the day after tomorrow,' Colly told the captain. '*Mezzogiorno, doppodomani.*'

'*Va bene, signore,*' said the skipper.

Though discreet, the skipper was curious. His eyes begged for explanations. But Colly said no more.

'We shall see if they rise to the bait,' said a man in a small dark office in Antalya.

'And if they do?'

'Then they are the persons in whom Mustafa Algan Bey is interested. If they do not rise to the bait, then, of course, they will go their way in peace, followed by such good wishes as the Koran instructs us to bestow on travellers.'

'If they do, as you put it, rise to your bait?'

'Then I have devised a wonderfully simple way to destroy them, the evidence, and their friends.'

Colly and Jenny came ashore early in the morning, with a small amount of hand baggage. They took a horse-drawn cab to the bus-park, a large, dusty, teeming, noisy, confusing area on the edge of the city, the caravanserai of modern Turkey, where nearly every journey to or from Antalya stopped or started. They had already bought tickets to Finike, from one of the little private bus companies which competed for the local trade. There seemed to be business for all the companies, and more, as every bus they had seen was always packed.

Their own bus was no exception. Half Antalya seemed to want to go that very day to Finike, or to one of the very few places on the way there. Every seat was filled. Down the central gangway more people were crammed, on the floor or on little stools – as many people as could be squeezed into the space. There was an immense quantity of the most miscellaneous baggage inside the bus; on the roof, under a tarpaulin, there was a mountain of bundles and cases.

It seemed to Jenny that there was hardly a trace, among these jam-packed Turks, of the apathetic fatalism which would have gripped a similar crowd in India: which would have rendered the Indians able to bear unbearable discomfort, but rendered them incapable of any action to lessen their discomfort. On the other hand, there was hardly a trace of the rude, sullen, whining, grumbling spirit which would have filled the bus in Western Europe, in France or Belgium or Germany or Britain.

The bus started northwards, as though to make the huge journey to Istanbul, but turned off to the west. It began to climb steeply, the road twisting in an endless series of hairpin bends among pine-trees. Parties of nomads were the only other users of the road – flocks of sheep and long-haired goats, a few pack camels and donkeys, a cluster of related families. The road climbed above the tree line, into a world of bare rock and thin scrub and, here and there, like strange green lakes, the upland pastures of the nomadic herdsmen.

They stopped, briefly, in a drab little town called Korkuteli, which was given some charm by the army of tall poplars which surrounded it. They were the other side of the Bey Mountains now; when they went on it was into a huge flat valley, at 4,000 feet, with the mountains rising ferociously to the east beyond rolling oceans of pastureland.

They stopped, for lunch, at a more considerable place called Elmali, clean and cobbled, with a thin minaret beside a fat mosque, and the streets dominated by the snowcapped tops of the mountains.

'Means "Appleville",' murmured Colly, 'which figures. I never saw so many apple trees.'

'Nice place,' said Jenny. 'We'd better sight-see. We've got an hour.'

They strolled, as the town's rare tourists would, up the steep, narrow backstreets behind the mosque. Ancient houses leaned against each other, with storks sitting on their chimneys, and there were trees and running water.

They emerged onto open hillside, and into an army of gnarled apple trees. Beyond and above the orchards there was scrubby, stony ground, seamed by several tiny streams. There, packed together, brilliantly red and pink, were acres upon acres of poppies.

'Heigh ho,' said Colly.

'You know what those are not?' said Jenny. 'They're not the ordinary weeds.'

'No. What's different?'

'Colour, for a start. Listen. Think. All the wild poppies we've seen, everywhere we've been, are dark red. Sort of a solid, hot, dark red. All exactly the same. Surely these are lighter, brighter. More a pillarbox. The ones that are red. Some are pink. Who ever heard of a wild pink poppy in Turkey?'

'I don't know,' said Colly. 'Are you telling me there's no such thing as a wild pink poppy in Turkey?'

'No. I don't know. I just don't think these are wild.'

'Neither do I, as a matter of fact, but for a different reason. The way they're growing. In nature, there has to be a terrific variation in the density seeds arrive on a piece of ground. Places they'll get blown away or washed away, places they'll lie in a goddam drift, places they'll throttle other vegetation, places just a plant or two will struggle up through something else.'

'Well, there's whatever you said here. Variation in density.'

'Sure, but not very much. This stuff wasn't sown in rows, obviously, or out of a machine, it was broadcast by hand. But look over there.'

'More poppies. Dark crimson. Not pink. Wild ones. Weeds.'

'Sown every which way. Seeds just landed where they

140

happened to land, and germinated if they happened to germinate. Which did Şefik's look like?'

'This lot,' said Jenny instantly. 'No pink ones, that I remember, but otherwise like this lot.'

'Then pick a little bouquet, darling. And I guess, when we get back to the bus, you'd better simper girlishly.'

A man who looked like a superior mechanic had a place in the gangway of the bus. He squatted on his toolbag. A friend in dirty overalls was with him; also a young boy, a spidery child of about nine.

The superior mechanic watched as the ill-favoured Swiss girl climbed, after her ridiculous father, into the bus. She held an armful of poppies, which were already beginning to droop. Her poppies included pink blossoms as well as pillarbox red ones.

The superior mechanic glanced at his companion, and made an idle remark about bait.

They went on through wheat country, flattish, still high, well watered, with snow capped mountains always limiting the plateau to the east. Then the valley narrowed. Mountainsides pressed right up to the sides of the road, which wriggled between them. It was hard work for the driver. The road descended steeply. Far below it, a river called the Başgöz spurted out of the mountainside and rushed towards the sea, fed by sidestreams and cataracts.

The effect was purely Alpine – swirling river, massed pine trees, steep hillsides, distant snows, clean sweet air, a sense of grandeur and remoteness. Except that, instead of Alpine plants, there were millions of poppies. Some were raggedly self-sown, smallish, dark crimson. Some were more evenly spread over cleaner ground, their massed colour coming to an abrupt end, pink here and there relieving the general vermilion.

'Some of these too?' murmured Jenny, her voice

141

drowned for all but Colly by the driver's cassette which was bellowing a lachrymose popular song.

'Yeah. I guess we should.'

'You know, as far as we know Mustafa Algan didn't come up here at all.'

'I'll bet he did.'

'He went down the coast by boat.'

'And took a trip inland.'

'How?'

'Probably in a Posta. Post Office jeep that takes passengers. You'll have to stop this driver, darling, little as he wants to stop.'

'Another fit?'

'I guess so. It's no good just fainting, or vomiting, he wouldn't stop for that.'

'This had better be a maxi-fit.'

'Hit 'er, kid.'

Jenny began to look very ill and strange, attracting glances from nearby passengers. Colly's face meanwhile grew more and more concerned, as though he could read too well the signal he was getting.

Jenny hit it. Her legs shot out straight, her back arched, her mouth gaped in an agonised silent scream, her eyes swivelled so that only the whites showed, and then she let out the awful high drone of the bad epileptic fit.

The driver stopped. He was reluctant to do so, but the public opinion of the bus was too strong for him. Colly scrambled down. A dozen people helped him get Jenny out into the fresh air. She was still as rigid as a poker. Colly and his new friends carried her a short way from the roadside. Presently she relaxed. Her eyelids flickered. She evidently felt a little weak and disoriented, but she was all right.

The bus had almost wholly emptied. Its passengers stood in a huge circle round Jenny, Colly, and two elderly peasant women who were credited with knowledge of medicine. The passengers had too much

142

instinctive courtesy to press close, to gawp ghoulishly; but they were interested, truly concerned, and anxious to be of help in any way. Jenny, looking round dazedly, was aware of this goodwill. She felt ashamed to have abused it by pretending.

On the way back to the bus, Colly and Jenny, between them, contrived to pick a few poppies. Nobody saw this, except two men and a bright-eyed boy who were expecting it and looking for it.

Finike had a harbour, with a breakwater which was also the quay. Colly thought it was deep enough for the *Uccello Bianco*. A few fishing boats were tied up to the quay, but there would be room for the yacht.

The town was small and friendly. Though evidently not rich, it caught good fish and grew good oranges; the best of the latter, Colly heard, went all the way to Smyrna for export, and thence, perhaps, all the way to Switzerland, where the unfortunate daughter of M. Marais could derive only benefit from eating them.

The nearest ancient site was a place called Limyra, about seven miles to the north east. It was largely ignored by the guidebooks; as far as Colly could gather it was totally uninteresting. Perhaps, all the same, it had given Mustafa Algan his excuse to come to this out-of-the-way little port.

There were three hotels, all small, none with restaurants, none full. They chose one which offered a shower-bath, and which had an available bedroom with only two beds in it. (Most hotels in small Turkish towns – those graded Third Class – have half a dozen beds in every room.)

They had red mullet, goat's-milk cheese, and a variety of excellent fruit and nuts in a tiny restaurant on the harbour. By ten in the evening the town was asleep and so were they.

The *Uccello Bianco* chugged gingerly into the harbour shortly before noon the next day. A leadsman was in the bows, and the skipper was watching the echo-sounder. There was water enough. The big white motor yacht caused high excitement; the quay was suddenly thronged. The people evidently expected that an Onassis or an Elizabeth Taylor would come ashore from the yacht. There was general disappointment when, instead, the foreign father and daughter – amiable but uninteresting people – went aboard.

Their small amount of hand-baggage went aboard with them. Invisible inside the bags were sheaves of wilted red and pink poppies.

The porthole of Jenny's cabin gave onto the quay. She glanced through it, idly, as she came into her cabin, followed by a deckhand with her case. It was not at all astonishing to see, among all the chattering and curious bystanders, a few faces familiar from the bus. Their fellow-passengers felt, no doubt, a kind of proprietary interest in the foreign girl who had had a fit in their midst, thus giving all of them something to talk about for months. They were intrigued by the yacht, and concerned to see her safely aboard it, as they had been concerned to see her safely back in their bus.

Colly came into Jenny's cabin with her sponge-bag, which a boy had brought from the hotel. Following Jenny's eye, he glanced out of the port-hole.

'All looking this way,' he said. 'I guess they're hoping you're gonna strip off ... Hey, did you see that?'

'See what?'

'The way that guy took his cap off and put it on again. Kind of a mannerism.'

'Not very rare. My Papa does it.'

'I don't think that's him, darling. I don't *think* it is. But it's a face I know.'

'People off the bus,' said Jenny.

'Yeah? The one I mean? The tall clean-shaven guy with a kind of carpet-bag? Was he on the bus?'

'I think so. I'm not sure. Why?'

'I met him in Antalya three days ago.'

'So?'

'So he wasn't dressed like that. Not a bit like that.'

'Nor were you, I daresay. So?'

'So I would never have recognised him, if he hadn't taken his cap off, just half off, and kind of wiggled it and put it back on. He hasn't just changed, he's in disguise.'

'So?'

'So he's the one who told me about all the beautiful poppies up there in the mountains.'

Jenny pondered for a moment, sitting on her bunk with her chin on her fists. She said, 'Then just possibly we've walked into a trap.'

'Again.'

'Yes. Again. I'm glad. We couldn't tail that big brute in a vast place like Smyrna, but surely we can keep an eye on your chum in a little dump like this?'

'Check. You cover yourself up with a rusty black bedsheet smelling of garlic, and I'll cover myself up with a big moustache smelling of garlic— '

'And your chum will be certain we're on board here— '

'Yeah. Because he saw us get on, and he won't see us get off. I hope.'

As darkness fell, a mist came in from the sea, or down from the mountains, and hid the stars. There was no moon; there was no wind. It was a pitch-black night. It was a good night for leaving the yacht unseen.

Jenny and Colly were sure the yacht was being watched. They were sure they could cheat the watchers. There was commotion above, in the saloon and on the afterdeck, to distract the watchers and hide other sounds. To the strains of loud music from a radio, Jenny and Colly slipped over the side of the yacht into a small rubber dinghy. They paddled it gently, through inky water, into the middle of the little fishing fleet. Then they were on the quay, among people who could not have seen them get there. Jenny was a hobbling old witch, with bandaged feet and mittenned hands, in an enveloping black yashmak. Colly was a seedy labourer with a moustache like a chimney-sweep's largest brush.

The rubber dinghy was pulled gently back to the yacht by a thin black nylon cord.

The newcomers on the quay idly joined the idlers already there. After a few minutes they confirmed that the *Uccello Bianco* was indeed being watched, tactfully, by someone who was not altogether an idler.

There was something to watch, too – some kind of celebration, partly under cover in the saloon, partly under the sky on the afterdeck. Music still blared; candles flamed benignly in the still air; there was a girlish laugh; there were guffaws, and jolly shouts in a strange language.

Colly blessed the forethought that had provided him with a discreet rogue for a skipper. It was lucky that the skipper was also a gleeful play-actor, and that one of the crew could produce an effective falsetto giggle.

Jenny and Colly settled themselves to watch the watcher. They would sit on his tail until they learned something. What they then did depended on what they learned. The man, in Antalya, had presumably received orders, presumably from Istanbul or Smyrna, presumably by some other means than post or telephone. Other means presumably meant a messenger. Messengers were visible. So much was likely. It was impossible to guess further. It was a question of following contacts along a chain until they led somewhere that helped Sandro; with the cross-bearing, hopefully, of the analysis of the poppies.

Meanwhile it was lucky there were two of them. One of the two could, at any moment, act as liaison with the yacht – could fetch things they needed from it, give orders to the skipper, send it off posthaste to Italy to have the poppies analysed, or to get a message to Sandro in Smyrna. As long as there were two of them, and the yacht was there, they needed no money with them, no

146

spare clothes or any baggage; they had a radio telephone; they could make a quick getaway. And as long as there were two of them, one could always go to sleep.

Their man had friends. This became evident. But, in the dark, they could not see the friends. One was a young boy.

The false party on the yacht came to a ragged end. Candles were blown out, lights switched off, music silenced. The watcher turned away; he strolled along the quay and into the town. Jenny and Colly followed, alert for the watcher's friends.

Jenny watched half the night while Colly slept; Colly watched the rest of the night while Jenny slept. It was no hardship to spend a night under the sky, outside a little house on the edge of Finike, in the balmy south Turkish air.

In the morning their subject – the tall clean-shaven man who sometimes carried a carpet-bag – sauntered, very early, back towards the harbour. He was a man with nothing to do. He sat drinking strong tea out of a glass, at the gazino, the open-air café, by the harbour. He watched the yacht, without seeming to do so, and drank glass after glass of tea.

It was not obvious that he had relieved another watcher, but it was probable.

Some time in the morning, Colly imagined, the skipper would start the big twin diesels of the *Uccello Bianco*. He would run them long enough to ensure that the batteries were at full charge, since every comfort of the yacht, as well as its safety, depended on the batteries.

Sure enough, soon after eight-thirty the engineer went to the cockpit. He had only to turn two keys and press two buttons.

Idly, Colly waited for the gentle thud of the diesels.

The explosion seemed to lift the *Uccello Bianco* clear out of the water.

Chapter 10

It seemed to Colly that there were two explosions – a small one, sharp, percussive, then a big one, slower, awesome, bursting the yacht outwards like an over-inflated children's balloon.

It figured. A stick of dynamite, or something equally convenient and portable, was detonated electrically when the engineer turned the ignition switch. That first explosion blew the diesel vapour and then, in a continuous reaction, lit the oil in the engines and the pumps and the pipes and the tanks.

Dense greasy smoke belched from the wreckage. Flames in the water licked at what was left of the *Uccello Bianco*.

The blast had thrown the little fishing-boats into each other. A few were smashed to pieces, none undamaged. There had been half a dozen people on the quay, some well away from the explosion but some near it. They all went down and stayed down. It was unlikely that all of them were dead, but it was not impossible. Windows were blown out all round the harbour. People were screaming. Many were cut by flying glass and other splinters. There was mess and panic and blood, and over everything the stinking black smoke from the burning diesel-oil.

'There's cons and a few pros,' said Colly.

'I can only see cons,' said Jenny glumly. 'Skipper and crew dead. Other people dead, locals on the jetty. The yatch in bits. Our clothes gone, passports, money

148

everything. Radio telephone gone – no chance of making any contact with anybody. Poppies gone, evidence that might have helped Sandro.'

'Yeah. I don't claim the pros outweigh that lot. But we're alive. We know who did this. It's getting clearer why he did it. We have a few clothes. I have some money. We have guns. And above all, baby, the opposition think we're dead.'

'What now? I'm too groggy to think straight.'

'Me too, but let's try. One thing we have to do is get some more of these goddam poppies, the fancy ones we think somebody planted. They *do* seem to be at the centre of this whole thing. Christ knows why, or what they're for, but there it is. We have to pick some more, and somehow we have to get them analysed.'

'We could hire a donkey. Two donkeys.'

'Donkey, bus, posta, no problem. No problem about getting to the Flanders fields up there. *But* we have to keep tabs on our friend.'

'One of us goes picking flowers, one sits and watches Arthur. I think it's your turn to pick flowers.'

'Yeah.' said Colly, 'but suppose Arthur hauls his freight while the poppy-picker is up yonder in the mountains?'

'Then the non-poppy-picker goes with him.'

'Then we lose contact.'

'Not for ever. Look, stupid. I go picking poppies. I come back. I find you've disappeared, and I find Arthur's disappeared. I deduce you've gone off with Arthur. I sit tight, spending the money you've given me— '

'I've given you money?'

'Of course. Don't let's forget *that*. I wait here, knowing you know that this is where I am. As long as I stay put, we *don't* lose contact.'

'It's terrible. If I'm on Arthur's tail he may take me to Istanbul or any goddam place. So I'm all alone, trying to keep a twenty-four hour tail on my own, in a strange place, which is impossible. And you're sitting here useless, and not very decorative either ... It won't do, baby. Staying close to Arthur has to be the first priority. For the both of us. For a while. Then we'll see where we're at.'

'I suppose Arthur will go back to Antalya?'

'I imagine so. He'll want to report to somebody how clever he was.'

'Claim a reward?'

'Nothing more likely. Nobody kills that many people for free.'

'Ugh. Did you see the child with the eye knocked out?'

'We know a little more,' said Colly. 'We really do.'

'Yes. But, oh God, at what a cost.'

Finike was in a turmoil. It was easy to watch the clean-shaven man they had called Arthur. They identified his companion, who wore dirty overalls, and had with him an active, bright-eyed small boy.

'That kid,' murmured Colly, 'is maybe how they got the bomb on board the *Uccello*. Could have gone down a ventilator.'

'Blimey,' said Jenny. 'Oliver Twist.'

'Yeah. I wonder what gave them that idea?'

Both the men they were watching seemed entirely unemployed. But they attracted no attention in the shocked confusion of the town, which was concerned only with its damage, its dead and injured, and the horrible mess in its harbour.

'What are they waiting for?' asked Jenny.

'A message,' said Colly. 'Another guy, I guess.'

'We could have got the poppies and come back three times over, by now.'

'I know it. It's maddening. It can't be helped.'

And then, on the fourth day after the explosion, another man came. He arrived in a Bedford truck. He parked the truck near the harbour, and went straight to the gazino where the clean-shaven man was drinking, as he spent nearly all his time doing, glass after glass of strong tea. The newcomer sat down with the clean-shaven man after a brief, almost perfunctory greeting. They were joined shortly afterwards by the man in dirty overalls, but not by the small boy. It was not, perhaps, a conversation suitable for small boys. The three men spoke earnestly and long, in low voices. Jenny tried to lip-read, but her rudimentary Turkish was not up to it. From time to time, as they talked, the men glanced at the wreckage of the *Uccello Bianco* which stuck up out of the water of the harbour. There was satisfaction in the face of the clean-shaven man. He had done something he was proud of. This would not have been visible to a stranger. His security was not so lax that he showed his feelings to the world. His satisfaction was visible, though, to someone who was observing him minutely, and had been doing so for days, and who knew all his mannerisms and the various expressions of his face.

The newcomer was neatly dressed in an indeterminate lower-middle-class style – a dark suit, quite clean, a white shirt buttoned to the neck but worn without a tie. He was the same age as the other men – perhaps thirty-seven or forty – with a strong, weatherbeaten face deeply lined each side of the mouth, a small moustache, big-boned hands, a look of animal power and perhaps passion close below the respectable exterior. He looked a man who went armed and could use his weapons. All three did: but the newcomer was the one Jenny least wanted to take on.

Jenny, peeping through a slit in her enveloping, rusty-black yashmak, watched the three at their table at the pleasant little open-air gazino. It became clear to her that the newcomer was the chief of the three. The clean-shaven man was the superior of the man in overalls, but the newcomer with the respectable, dangerous look was superior to them both. There was no kowtowing, no obvious deference, but after half an hour the pecking order was detectable.

151

If the three separated, Jenny thought, the newcomer was the man to follow, if possible.

Early the following morning, the clean-shaven man, the man in dirty overalls and the boy came down to the harbour with a collection of bags, parcels and cardboard boxes. It was their luggage.

Colly nodded to himself, aware again of professionalism. The clean-shaven man he had briefly met in Antalya would have had a smart plastic suitcase. He disguised himself in depth. Colly was sure that every single thing in his luggage would be consistent with the part he was now playing, of a superior mechanic who had come to Finike to repair a pump or a generator. But no one had told him about his mannerism with the peak of his cap.

The tatty luggage went into the back of the truck.

'Well now,' said Colly, 'who goes? Who stays? If they all go, who travels in the back of that truck? If somebody's in the back, where do *we* go?'

The problem was not unexpected, but, for all its predictability, it threatened to be insoluble.

The solution lay not in anything which Colly or Jenny did or devised, but in the way of life of rural Turkey. It became known in the streets of Finike that the truck was going, after its driver had drunk some tea and eaten a moderate number of the delicious local oranges, to Antalya, by way – the only way – of Elmali and Korkuteli. Twenty people instantly surrounded the truck, with very small sums of money in their hands, demanding or beseeching lifts.

The man in the white shirt laughed, and opened the back of his truck. The twenty sprang aboard, old women showing amazing agility, old men falling back but struggling forward again, luggage pouring on.

Two travellers not generally known to the others were in the very midst of the crowd. One was a very old peasant woman, shrouded from head to foot in musty black to an extent no longer usual, even in remote

152

places, in modern Turkey. Her voice was cracked and unintelligible owing to senility; her misshapen hands were concealed by woollen gloves, and her ancient feet by cocoons of dirty bandages. With this ill-smelling crone was her son or grandson, a scruffy, grubby, ordinary workman, with ordinary cloth cap, baggy trousers and cheap shoes, and ordinary ferocious black moustache.

Colly did what they had more than once done before, to cope with a language he did not know well or speak fluently. He developed an appalling stammer.

Mother and son (perhaps grandmother and grandson) had both, it seemed, been touched by the hand of Allah. It was very sad. But it was not as sad as what had happened at Finike when the foreign yacht blew up.

The truck left in the middle of the morning. In the front were the man in the white shirt, his two friends, and the boy. In the back were twenty humble people who were travelling more cheaply than on the bus. It was crowded, uncomfortable, bumpy and friendly in the back of the truck.

Picking poppies – being seen picking poppies – was presumably how they had nudged the enemy into blowing up the *Uccello Bianco*, killing her skipper and crew, killing and maiming some of the people of Finike, and breaking a great deal of the town's glass. The men who had seen Jenny pick the poppies were now in the front of the truck. They might not be as watchful as before, because of what they thought they had achieved with their murderous bomb: but they had not been struck blind. If they saw anything as weird as an old peasant woman picking poppies – unusual poppies, some pink, not quite like the ordinary wild poppies – they were pretty certain to do sums in their heads.

In, Colly reminded himself, their highly professional heads.

But poppies had to be picked – had to be picked, and then somehow sent away for analysis. The latter was another problem for another day. Immediately, poppies

153

had to be picked. The truck had to be stopped, and in the right place.

It might stop in Elmali. This was likely but uncertain. It would be madness to rely on it. It might stop in Elmali, but only for a few minutes, long enough for the people to get a glass of tea or of raki, not long enough for a stroll out into the apple orchards and beyond to the drifts of poppies on the hillside.

The truck had to be stopped: but another fit was out of the question. Any kind of sudden illness was probably out of the question, whether Jenny suffered it or Colly, because it would remind the cold-eyed men in the front of the truck of the events of a few days before.

Colly decided to fall out of the truck.

A young woman had already been wretchedly and noisily sick over the tailboard of the truck, to which she clung, sobbing and retching, like a miserable steerage passenger clinging to the rail of an immigrant ship. Trembling, this girl collapsed yellow-faced amongst her clucking family, having set Colly a useful precedent. He crawled to the tailboard and took her place, hanging limply over it, clinging and moaning.

Twice before in his life Colly had used, in moments of crisis, an ability he had to throw up deliberately. Once was during his schooldays, when he had evaded a well-earned whipping by producing his breakfast on the carpet in the headmaster's study. The second time was many years later, on a yacht in the Caribbean, in the company of a kidnapped girl and two blackmailing homosexual gangsters*. The moment had come – was imminently due to come – for a third performance.

The glorious countryside unrolled behind the truck as they climbed up the tortuous valley of the Başgöz river – snow-capped peaks of the Bey Daği, deep crimson splashes of wild poppies, acres of the vivid yellow

*This tense and ambiguous episode is described in *The Man with the Tiny Head*, by the same author.

154

blossom of the box-thorn. It was not difficult to feel sick. The dreadful noise made by the young woman had been enough, almost, to turn the stomach. There was something vertiginous and upsetting in looking down at the road pouring itself out backwards between the rear wheels of the truck. The truck laboured up the steeper sections of the road in low gear, exhaust fumes filling the air round Colly's head. It was not difficult to feel sick, but it was too soon to be sick.

Then Colly saw what he was looking for. He saw poppies. The first of the primmer, tidier poppies, the pink and vermilion poppies. He began at once to be sick, noisily and protractedly. He pushed himself far out over the tailboard, moaning, making the same awful noises as the girl had made, but making them louder.

Poppies grew close to the road. The nearest were only yards from the edge of the road, from the wheels of the truck.

Colly was shaken by a paroxysm, as though being sick was affected, like speech, by the appalling stammer he had assumed. Hanging far out over the tailboard, he shifted his centre of gravity a further crucial inch, and tumbled over.

He knew that no one in the truck was in a position to see him hit the road. No one had wanted to share the tailboard with a man being disgustingly sick. Unobserved, he landed on his hands, bending his arms as shock-absorbers. He tucked his chin on his chest and let himself roll on his shoulders. This was a judo fall which would have prevented him from hurting himself even if the truck had been travelling much faster. The roll took him off the road and right to the edge of the nearest patch of poppies.

There was a scream like a steam-whistle from the back of the truck. Jenny. All the other people in the truck shouted to the driver, and all those nearest the front banged on the back of the cab. The truck stopped thirty yards from where Colly lay. The clean shaven man jumped down from the cab and ran back, and the truck began to reverse.

By this time Colly had picked a handful of poppies and rolled them in an oily and tattered handkerchief. He secreted this in the baggy seat of his trousers. It was not a place likely to be searched.

Colly knew that if by chance he was searched by these people, and they found the poppies, then he was dead.

People surrounded him. Some prodded him. He stammered at them, gasping and incomprehensible. It was established that he was slightly scratched and bruised, but not otherwise injured. This was considered a miracle. The consensus in the truck was that Allah had intervened, since the victim had been sufficiently afflicted by his stammer.

Colly was restored to his mother or grandmother in the back of the truck; she seemed unable to believe that he was alive, let alone unhurt, and set up a wail as for the dead. She was quietened at last, and the truck proceeded.

Colly did not think he was suspected by the men in the front of the truck.

Colly had been wise to go poppy picking when and as he did. He saw no more masses of the special poppies anywhere near the road. It seemed to him that, altogether, there were fewer of those poppies than he remembered seeing from the bus when they made the journey in the opposite direction.

Jenny confirmed this, gabbling softly like a senile bird from under her frowsty yashmak. 'I think they've harvested some,' she said.

Inspecting the hillside as they bumped up the gorge, Colly became sure she was right. There had been some bare patches, caused perhaps by the barrenness of the ground, perhaps by the removal of vegetation. Now there were more. They were not at all noticeable, to any casual eye. He would not have noticed them himself, with his city-bred eye. But Jenny had been brought up in the countryside – not this one, but obeying many of the same rules – and she was deeply versed in the small changes which countrymen can see about them.

There were more bare patches. There were, here and there, fewer poppies. Yet there were still, here and there, huge numbers of poppies in dense carpets of brilliant colour. Why were they not harvested too?

It came to Colly that the growers of the poppies had sown them – if it was really to be believed that red and pink poppies were deliberately sown – not all at once, but in successive lots, as a gardener will sow lettuce and broad beans weekly, so that he will not have his whole crop on top of him at one moment, but a convenient supply over a period. Maybe the poppy seed had been sown once a week, or once every two weeks, so that only a modest amount had to be harvested at any given moment ...

Yes, but harvest these poppies? These pink and red poppies? It seemed they were sown. It seemed they were harvested. But *why?*

The truck did stop in Elmali, but only for a short time. All the travellers in the back of the truck were politely asked to get out, while some boxes were loaded in. They were boxes of apples. It was a consignment of very special Elmali apples, going to the hotels and restaurants of Antalya.

'Only,' murmured Jenny to Colly, 'the apples here aren't ripe yet.'

'My God,' grunted Colly, 'are you sure? Those old trees we saw, just over there, the other day, they were groaning under goddam apples.'

'Take my word for it,' said Jenny.

'Okay,' said Colly, who knew he could safely do so.

'We must peek inside those crates.'

'Should be easy, once we start again.'

The apple crates came out of an ordinary barn beside an ordinary farmhouse at the edge of Elmali. They were carried to the truck by ordinary workmen, dressed exactly as was Colly in baggy trousers and cloth caps. The sides of the crates were slatted. Between the slats could be seen ordinary green apples.

'Apples,' grumbled Colly. 'Sure enough apples.'

'One layer of apples. Then what?'

The crates lined the floor of the truck. They were stacked to a height of three at the front, then two. Many more crates could easily have been put in the truck, but it seemed that this load was the whole consignment.

It was not a great quantity of apples for a town the size of Antalya, provincial capital and tourist centre. But it was a great quantity of unripe, inedible green apples.

None of the other travellers gave the apple crates a second look. None commented on them, except as tending to make the back of the truck still less comfortable than before. None of the travellers had so much as glanced at the pink and vermilion poppies, the unusual ones. Anatolian peasants are not interested in pretty weeds.

Most of the travellers had a glass of tea at a gazino near the house where the truck had stopped. Colly strolled idly back and forth, walking stiffly after his fall from the truck. He wanted a close look at the house and barn. He might have risked some vague, casual prying, if he had not already made himself desperately conspicuous. Innocent, he thought, but damned conspicuous.

For Jenny, cackling and senile, to explore the barn would be totally out of character. Her rôle required her to squat apathetically until the journey started again.

It was likely, anyway, that there was nothing to be seen in house or barn. Everything that needed looking at was probably already in the crates, under the layers of green apples. They were the objective.

The passengers heaved themselves and each other into the back of the truck, and festooned themselves over the apple crates. A few passengers were staying in Elmali, but their places were taken by others. There were,

158

perhaps, more arrivals than departures; the truck was more crowded and uncomfortable, and it was less possible to do anything unseen by all the other people in the truck.

The truck started for Korkuteli, going at a good pace through the magnificent broad wheat-lands between the high mountains.

Colly and Jenny had very little space. People leaned against them and thrust against them, in perfect good-will, often apologetic. It was impossible for Colly to make any vigorous movement without a dozen people being instantly aware of it. Since they were friendly Anatolian peasants, the people would be curious as soon as they were aware. *What* was the man, afflicted by Allah with a mouth unable to make sounds of speaking, doing to the wooden planks on the top of the crate on which he was squatting? Removing them? In order to steal apples?

Colly did not know how the public opinion of the passengers would react to apple stealing. But he was very sure he did not want to be seen levering a plank off a crate.

The crates were made of much heavier timber than is usually used for fruit boxes. In Turkey, like everywhere else, the thinnest pieces of the cheapest wood form the slats which keep the fruit in the crate. But these apples had stout pine planks over them, and that for a journey of little over fifty miles. The packaging was out of all proportion to the value of the contents. It was ridiculous extravagance, if only apples were in the crates.

It was impossible for Colly to look more closely at the apples, or to search below them. The planks were nailed down with three or four nails each, at each end. It was conceivable that Colly could have levered off a plank with his knife blade, but he thought the knife blade would break first. He had no other tool. Even with a tool, it was inconceivable that Colly could get a plank off a crate unseen and unheard.

The weight of the planking was only one oddity in the packing of this fruit. Another was that the crates had been overfilled. The apples were jammed together, and the planks had been jammed down on top of them. When the planks had been hammered down, they had cut or bruised several of the apples in each crate. Those apples must be unsaleable. They would be thrown away, or given to children (to whom, green as they were, they would give stomach aches).

Unripe as they were, the cut and bruised apples exuded juice betwen the slats of the crates. The juice had a sharp, sweet, fruity smell, a delightful smell, quite strong. The back of the truck was full of the smell of bruised apples, fighting the smell of diesel fumes and tobacco and the clothes and teeth of the passengers.

The people of Elmali, famous apple growers, must be skilled in packing apples. It came to Colly that some of the people, this time, had used their skill in a new way. They had caused the apples to smell strong and delightful, by deliberately cutting and bruising them, in order to hide some other smell, just as the apples themselves hid whatever was below them in the crates.

The truck stopped at Korkuteli, after an uncomfortable hour and a half. All the passengers scrambled out and looked for a çayevi, a tea-house. The truck was suddenly deserted. No one was near it or looking at it. Colly lingered near the back of the truck. He stretched painfully, to explain, to anyone who might be looking, why he had not joined the trek to the tea-house. Jenny squatted, like a diseased animal, at the side of the road.

'All clear,' she murmured.

At this moment the clean-shaven man strode up. He glanced without interest at Colly and at Jenny, and climbed into the back of the truck. He sat among the crates, facing outwards, his hand in the pocket of his jacket.

He was guarding the crates, and he had a gun in his pocket and in his hand. He was like the man who had

160

guarded the carpets of Mustafa Algan, in the little closed truck outside Bursa. He was adopting the same routine because he worked for the same outfit.

Colly shrugged mentally, and walked slowly to the çayevi.

They climbed a little, then threaded interminable hairpins downhill towards the coast. Colly nearly went mad, sprawled on crates which he saw no way to see inside.

Something was being carried secretly, guiltily, from Elamli to Antalya. Sight of it was hidden. Smell of it was hidden. It was guarded by a man with a gun – a man who had already, with his friends, committed multiple murder because Jenny had been seen picking poppies.

Surely, surely, the contraband under the apples would answer questions. Explain the poppies, maybe. Explain Şefik Bozkurt's murder, maybe, and so save Sandro's life. And there was no way to see the contraband, no way to get answers to the questions. Colly nearly went mad, sprawled on the crates, inches from whatever lay below the oozing, innocent green apples.

They bumped down the granite-chip road, through cedars and resinous pines, and then through olive and orange groves. They came down onto the big main road, asphalted and busy, the beginning of the enormous journey to Istanbul. Smooth and fast they slid into Antalya a few minutes before sunset. The truck stopped. All the passengers climbed out, chatting and laughing and lugging their bundles. Colly and Jenny had to get out with the rest, for the man in the white shirt and the man in dirty overalls stood by the tail of the truck making sure that it was emptied.

The chance was lost.

When only the crates remained in the truck, the man in dirty overalls climbed in and sat on the crates, as his friend had done. His hand, like his friend's, was in his pocket. Colly wondered if he held the same gun, or whether they each had guns.

The man in the white shirt got under the wheel of his truck and started it. The truck disappeared round a corner.

'You left your toothbrush on board,' murmured Jenny from behind her shawls.

'So I did,' said Colly out of the side of his mouth.

He began to run after the truck making a gargling noise as though he were trying to shout through his stammer. There were sympathetic clucks from the kindly fellow passengers.

Colly reached the corner, panting. The truck had disappeared. He looked up a steep street, barely wide enough for the truck, going up the hillside from the harbour. Many alleys led off the street. The alleys led into other alleys, or into small courtyards of various peculiar shapes. Evening shadows were filling the street. There was a hum of voices and a strong smell of cooking – of resinous wood fires, roasting meat, baking. There was no sound of an engine.

Far up the street Colly saw a gleam of white. It was the white shirt of a man in a decent dark suit. The man was calling. Colly knew his voice. To his call came four men from an ancient, decrepit house leaning over the street: labouring men like those who had loaded the crates onto the truck. They followed the man in the white shirt into the mouth of an alley.

Colly hurried as inconspicuously as he could up the street. He shambled past the mouth of the alley. He saw what he expected to see: the crates being unloaded from the truck into a building, a sort of fruit-store or granary. The building had massive stone walls and a massive door. Colly was sure that once the door was locked the building could only be burgled with explosive. There would also be an armed guard on the crates as long as they were in the building.

Colly edged forward uncertainly, hardly visible in the

162

deep shadows of the alley, a labourer like any other. He did not want to be seen by three armed professional criminals to whom he had already, by falling out of the truck, made himself conspicuous.

But he wanted to know what was in the crates.

They were disappearing rapidly into the storehouse. Few were left on the truck. Colly's last chance was disappearing with the crates.

If a crate was dropped – dropped from a fair height, from the back of the truck, onto the cobbles of the alley – it would almost certainly burst. That was the only way a crate could be opened quickly, and all its contents spread about for Colly to see. One of the porters must drop one end of a crate as it was being lifted off the truck.

Colly needed a blowpipe and a dart, a compressed-air pistol, a sling-shot, a crossbow – anything which, silent and invisible, would give one of the porters such a sudden shock that he dropped the end of a crate. He had nothing like that. He had nothing, except his gun, that he could throw. He dared come no nearer. He dared not make any obvious, visible attack.

Two men were sliding the very last crate from the front of the truck to the tail. One jumped to the ground. The other pushed the crate out beyond the tail of the truck. The man on the ground took the weight.

Colly swore bitterly and helplessly.

Suddenly the man who was taking the weight of the crate cried out, clapping his hand to the back of his neck. He let the crate go. It crashed to the ground and burst.

Simultaneously there was a giggle close behind Colly. He spun round. Jenny stood there, in deep shadow, holding a small piece of fabric.

'My pants,' she murmured. 'Good strong elastic. Catapult. Good shot, yes? What's he dropped?'

Apples had burst out of the crate. They rolled all over the rough ground in the alley. Every one was an apple. There was nothing in the crate except apples.

Chapter 11

'What was it that afflicted Osman in the neck?' asked the man in the white shirt.

'He does not know,' said the clean-shaven man. 'He said it was as though he had been shot.'

'He was not shot.'

'Or stung by a bee.'

'He was not stung by a bee.'

'He did not *invent* a sudden sharp pain in the neck. I think. I saw him clap a hand to his neck, thus letting go of the box of apples.'

'Which were apples.'

'By the mercy of Allah, it was the box containing nothing but apples, for placing on top of all the other boxes.'

'By the mercy of Allah, and by dint of the forethought of Algan Bey.'

'I begin to believe,' said the clean-shaven man, 'that they are the same thing.'

'I,' said his friend, 'have always believed it.'

'Goddam apples,' said Colly.

'Something inside the apples?' suggested Jenny,

'No. They threw the whole lot out. They weren't interested in keeping them, and they don't care who sees them. They're just bruised green apples. If you want to cut them open and look inside, you can. They're lying all over the alley. They ran the truck over a few, squashed them into apple sauce. You can go look at that, too, if you want.'

'Those poppies you're carrying in your breeks. How do we get them analysed?'

'God knows. Like practically everything else, it's another problem for another day. We can't talk to anybody respectable, in confidence, until we have some clothes and some more dough— '

'We can't turn back into those awful Swiss again.'

'No. I guess that would be a little unhealthy.'

'I'm thankful to have got rid of that awful Monique, anyway.'

'I thought she suited you, darling. I seemed to see the real you for the first time.'

'No, this is the real me, an old bag in a yashmak, squatting in a gutter and smelling of drains ... I must say, I don't envy the analyst who finally does get to work on those poppies of yours, after they've been nestling in your crotch for a month ... I suppose we keep an eye on that shed, and go where the apples go? Even though they are just apples?'

'Yeah. I guess so. If we can. It's the only lead we have.'

'Nothing about Sandro's trial in the newspapers yet?'

'Nothing yet.'

Other small trucks pulled into the alley off the steep street above the harbour. Crates of produce of various kinds were unloaded into the storehouse – apricots, beans, carrots, figs.

It was impossible for Colly and Jenny to take a close look at the loads, or to repeat the manoeuvre with the catapult. It was impossible for them to get into the storehouse, where a man was always on guard and the walls and doors were impregnable.

Early one morning a bigger truck throbbed and spluttered in the street. It was too big to enter the alley. Crates were carried by the same four workmen, from the storehouse to the truck. Jenny, seeing the crates, pinched herself. She had seen scores of boxes of fruit and vegetables going into the store, until it must have been almost chock-full. Out of it came crates of machinery, planks nailed down all round, stencilled names and instructions on the planks. Some monstrous Turkish magic had converted apples and carrots into pistons and vacuum-pumps.

'Same merchandise, different labels,' murmured Colly.

'But the apples *were* apples.'

'The ones we saw.'

'Can we get a lift on this truck?'

'We can try.'

They tried and failed: together with a dozen other people, who heard that the truck was going to Konya, inland, 160 miles to the north-east. It was not probable that many of the people wanted to go all the way to Konya; they hoped to ride for a few lira to places on the way, to Manavgat, Akseki, Beyşehir. They found it difficult to accept that the truck was already overloaded, without passengers. All trucks were always overloaded.

The truck went off without any of the people. But in the back, sitting on the crates of machinery, was the man in dirty overalls, who kept his hand always in the pocket of his overalls. In the cab, with the driver, was the clean-shaven man. The driver himself was a newcomer, a fattish, swarthy man wearing an incongruous pearl-grey Homburg hat.

'We know where it's going,' said Colly. 'I guess we'd better go too.'

There were two bus routes to Konya. One, longer but reportedly on much better roads, went by Burdur and Isparta, keeping to the west of the westernmost spurs of the high Taurus mountains. The other took the road which, according to the reliable grapevine of the streets, the truck was taking.

Both buses started early the following morning. There was no means of leaving earlier. No railway came within one hundred miles of Antalya, and a charter light aircraft was far outside Colly's present character (which he had no immediate means of changing) and of the money he had with him. The delay was maddening. But the truck would not make fast time, loaded as it was, on the bad roads and steep gradients of the journey.

They discussed stealing a car, even a motorcycle. It was too risky. If they were caught, which was not at all unlikely, Sandro's conviction became certain. There were chances which normally they would have taken without a thought, which today they could not contemplate.

Their bus was an elderly Mercedes, dilapidated but powerful and very noisy. It was full to bursting when it started soon after the advertised time. It went briskly along the coast road to the east, past the antiquities they had dutifully visited, and turned inland beyond Manavgat. Immediately they were in the foothills of the Taurus, climbing steeply on a rough surface among superb pinewoods. The country was very beautiful and seemed utterly uninhabited.

They paused in Akseki, a little hill town with cultivation below and barren heights all round. The truck was there. It had broken down, or collected yet more cargo, or distributed some of its cargo. The clean shaven man and the man in the grey Homburg were having tea in a café. The man in dirty overalls squatted like a spider on the crates.

The bus left before the truck.

'A little worrying,' said Colly. 'I like a front tail, but only if I set my own tempo ...'

'We daren't leave the bus.'

'Nope.'

They chugged over the 5,000-foot pass of Irmasan, and they were deep in the southern Taurus, wild and empty and beautiful. The powerful old bus pounded along bad but adequate roads. Probably the truck was getting further and further behind. There was no stop, because there was nowhere to stop.

At last they did stop, at Beysehir, a rickety little town on the bank of an enormous lake.

167

The truck rumbled into Beysehir just as the bus rumbled out.

After seventy more miles they came to Konya, set in the midst of the interminable Anatolian plateau. They went at a dangerous speed through sleezy suburbs, perilously crossed a teeming market-place, and drew up in the city's bus park.

'Back to the edge of town,' said Colly.

'To see our friends in. Yes. But we may wait for hours. We may wait all night.'

'My guess is we will. We'll take turns sleeping. We have to, baby.'

'Yes,' agreed Jenny. 'But I don't have to like it.'

They were in a world completely different from the soft, lush Mediterranean coast – a high, austere place, with hot parched air and parched ground, which would be bitterly cold in winter. Also they were in a large, rich, populous city, a famous centre since Hittite times, full of important mosques and museums and antiquities: a far cry from the grubby and friendly simplicity of the little coastal towns.

They were, themselves, just as inconspicuous.

'This is one of the places Mustafa Algan came to,' said Colly suddenly.

'Yes. It's a carpet place.'

'He can come here openly, mosey around, buy carpets ...'

'Those crates came here too. Machinery which is really apples.'

'Apples which are maybe apples.'

'Or maybe something else. Something made of poppies.'

'Made,' said Colly, 'out of goddam red and pink poppies, which nobody ever made anything out of ... Jesus, that needle stuck in that groove for weeks, and we're no nearer knowing what goes on ...'

Colly bought a bicycle – an ancient bone-rattler, barely

roadworthy. He bought it from a man in the market who had injured his leg and could no longer use it. It was not expensive, but it made a considerable dent in the small sum of money Colly still had.

It was a godsend.

They waited, with the bicycle, just outside the dingy suburb of Konya on the road to Beyşehir. They waited all night, and most of the following morning. Towards noon, the familiar truck rumbled unhurriedly towards them. Colly followed it on his bicycle into the city, weaving perilously among the lawless cars and trucks and the donkeys and pedestrians in the streets.

The truck stopped in a back street. The man in the grey Homburg and the man in dirty overalls went into a small modern house. The clean shaven man was sitting on the crates of machinery, his hand in the pocket of his coat.

It was lunchtime. Colly was fairly sure the truck would be outside the house for an hour. It was a risk that had to be taken. He sped back to Jenny, who had herself hurried to their rendezvous outside a mosque. They went together to the house in the back street, Colly pushing his bicycle. The truck was still there. The man in overalls was now on guard.

The other men came out of the house and climbed into the cab of the truck.

'Off you go, darling,' said Jenny. 'See you at the mosque, some time next week I expect.'

'Yeah. I can probably see which road they take. But that's probably all I can do.'

It was all he could do. The truck took a bad road to the north. Colly followed it for a mile, but the chain fell off his bicycle.

'Nuts,' he said to Jenny later. 'Could be going north to Ankara, could be north-west to Akşehir. But it wasn't on the main Ankara road ...'

'I don't think it's going far,' said Jenny.

'Why?'

'I don't know. What is there near, to the north?'

169

'Looks like nothing but the most terrible empty hills. Absolutely dry and bleak and dead. But they must be going someplace ...'

Colly, using his stammer to hide the inadequacy of his Turkish, made innocent enquiries in the market-place. Ten kilometres north of Konya there was a small town called Sille. It was wholly without interest, he was told. There was nothing there. Once it had been an important staging-post for caravans from the east, but the railway to Konya bypassed it, and it had shrunk to poverty and unimportance. There were no factories there. There was no possible use there for crates of new machinery. There was no money there to buy machinery.

'We blew it,' said Colly. 'We should have got ourselves a car.'

'How?'

'Stolen one. Taken the chance. Presumably those guys didn't go to Sille, but someplace else. Maybe an isolated farm. As far as we're concerned they dropped off the edge of the world. I guess now we watch that house where the truck stopped. Or go back to Antalya and pick up the guy with the clean shirt. Or ...'

'Carpets,' said Jenny. 'Where do they make carpets here? Where would Mustafa Algan have gone?'

Innocent, stammered questions brought, at last, the answer.

The best carpets for very many kilometres around were made in small private houses in Sille.

The bus ride was brief but terrifying. Unimportant and poor as Sille had apparently become, the one daily bus there from Konya was as packed as all other Turkish buses. Even the Turkish passengers were shrill with complaint at the furious way the bus was driven. The bus itself seemed certain to fall to pieces at each bump in the bumpy road.

The country to the north of the city grew rapidly bleaker and bleaker. The hills were high, bare, ugly.

170

Sille itself was ugly and dirty, almost a ghost town. There were children begging in the streets, something Colly and Jenny had seen nowhere else in Turkey, even in the slums of Istanbul. There were poor, ragged children in other places, but they gave their poverty dignity by selling matches or bootlaces: they were not beggars but traders. The children of Sille were a nasty echo of Indian poverty, of Eygptian obsequiousness.

They saw the truck at once. It was parked near the scruffy little bus park at the edge of the town, outside a house in a dirty, rutted lane. The house was old, with bulging walls and high narrow windows, and a door as massive as that of the storehouse in Antalya. It was a bigger house than it looked at first, owing to extensions at the back; it was much bigger than the other houses in the squalid lane near the bus park.

'A load of machinery,' murmured Colly, 'in *there*?'

'We'd better peek.'

'Now?'

'Later.'

They found a dreadful little teashop from which they could just see the empty truck and the house.

Stammering, Colly asked about carpet making. He said he was ignorant owing to coming from a place where carpets were admired but not made; he would be interested to see the weaving of a carpet in this famous place.

Such a thing was impossible. Women and girls made all the carpets, in their own homes. They were very old-fashioned people in Sille. They were suspicious of strangers, and would not admit outsiders into their houses. The men of a house, also, would on no account permit an outsider to enter and watch their women at work. Other parts of Turkey, Konya itself, might have become infected with loose western ideas, but not Sille.

'Great cover,' said Colly. 'They're *expected* to do everything behind locked doors. Everybody works in secret. It might look funny someplace else, but here it looks normal, obeys the local rules.'

'Cover?' said Jenny. 'Yes. Okay. Cover for what?'

'For something, sure enough. We did a lot of guessing, but there's plenty we didn't invent. We'll go look. Later.'

Many hours later, in the gathering darkness, Jenny stood on Colly's shoulders and peeped in through one of the high narrow windows. It was the only window unshuttered. The room inside was high and narrow, like its single window. It was well lit by two oil lamps. Against the wall, facing Jenny, stood a loom. Two women were weaving a carpet, a beautiful, intricate design in rich dark colours. They were working to a coloured pattern tucked into the cords above their work. They threaded lengths of coloured wool through the cords, snipped off the ends with knives, and from time to time pushed the wool down with wooden-toothed combs. The women worked with great speed and expertness, in total silence. It was fascinating to watch, almost hypnotic. Both women were heavily veiled. They kept their backs to the window.

There was nothing in the room except the loom, the low bench on which the two women sat, the roll of completed carpet under the loom, the oil lamps, and the bunches of coloured wool. There were no other people, no other furniture, no signs of crates or machinery.

'What they do in there,' said Jenny, 'is make carpets.'

'You saw one room. There's a lot of the house you didn't see.'

Nor could they see any more of the house. There were other high, narrow windows. They were shuttered. Lights gleamed behind the shutters. There were people in the house, murmuring voices. It was impossible to hear what the people said; it was impossible to guess how many people there were, or what they were doing.

They watched the house for three days, and the empty truck parked outside it. Time crawled. They agreed that it was the best and only thing to do, but it was very boring and frustrating.

172

An upright elderly man with a big moustache came in and out of the house a few times daily. The man in the grey Homburg and the clean shaven man came out, went to a café, and returned. They attracted no notice from the despondent, apathetic people of Sille; nor did Colly and Jenny.

'Boxes of fruit turn into boxes of machinery,' said Colly fretfully. 'What in hell do boxes of machinery turn into? What in hell has any of this to do with goddam poppies, or Sandro, or us?'

'Ah,' said Mustafa Algan in the Great Bazaar in Istanbul. 'You temper your bad news with good, which is both courteous and prudent. Putting it another way, you vitiate your good news with bad. Another shipment of seed at Ortahisar is *good*. But the obduracy of the Russian who supplies the seed ...'

'It will not be easy to make a direct appeal to him, beyeffendi.'

'We do not do things because they are easy, but because they are necessary or profitable. A message must go to Kayseri, and thence to our friend in Ortahisar. From there, by the route he knows, to the far east, and to our Kurdish friend. From there to the Armenian courier, and from him to the supplier who says he can no longer supply us. And we shall hear no more of this nonsense.'

'There is more bad news, beyeffendi. The man and the girl were not on board the yacht when Süleyman, using your elegant device of the small boy, caused the explosion at Finike.'

'You grieve me. Is this certain?'

'Virtually. All the other bodies were recovered. The captain of the yacht had presented himself, as he was obliged to do, to the port authorities at Antalya and Finike, giving details of his crew and passengers. The bodies of the crew were recovered and identified. They numbered only the number of the crew, and did not include a woman. The women who were killed on the quayside were identified by their families.'

'Then the threat continues. How irritating. All our friends must, all over again, be ... Or have we reason to believe that these two have been identified?'

'We think so, beyeffendi. Among the persons whom Süleyman took as passengers on the truck from Finike to Antalya, as camouflage for his cargo, were two persons who— '

'Were not known to the others, even in so small a place as Finike?'

'That is exactly right. A man and a woman. The woman, as described, appeared to be extremely old, but nothing of her was actually visible on account of veils, shawls, gloves, bandages ...'

'Her voice?'

'She merely whined and dribbled, it is reported. Nothing could be understood of anything she said.'

'Oho! And he? The man? Could he be ...?'

'He bore no obvious resemblance to the seeming Swiss. Of course, we would not expect him to do so, if he is in truth the one we seek. Nor to the American whom you saw here. He was the right size, however.'

'His voice?'

'Also strange. Allah had afflicted him with a stammer so severe that persons had the greatest difficulty in understanding him.'

'For that,' said Mustafa Algan, 'I feel unaffected admiration. What an ingenious method of concealing a foreign accent, an incomplete mastery of a language.'

'This man fell out of the back of the truck, when apparently vomiting, while it was in motion. He fell on the road, but was not hurt.'

'Then he is expert at falling out of trucks.'

'He fell near poppies. Our poppies.'

'Then why did he live another minute?'

'Süleyman and the others did not know, then, that the Swiss father and daughter were not killed in the explosion.'

174

'I see. Did he pick any poppies?'

'That is not certain. He was, for a moment, out of anyone's sight.'

'But he was searched?'

'I regret to report, beyeffendi, that he was not.'

'And now? The stammering man, and the invisible old woman?'

'Have been lost sight of, beyeffendi.'

'All the curses of hell on the incompetent idiots who pretend to serve me.'

'...*But* a man with a severe stammer, a stranger, was asking if he might observe the weaving of carpets—'

'Where?'

'At Sille. In a teashop, a hundred yards from Fikret's house, outside which was stationed the larger truck of Süleyman.'

'Alláhallah! I suppose by now they have broken into and inspected my factory.'

'They have not done so yet. At least, they had not done so, when the last message arrived from Konya. They *could* not, beyeffendi.'

'It seems there is little they cannot do. I am not accustomed to dealing with persons of such resource, especially English girls ... Since they have been reported in Sille, they are now under observation? Or dead?'

'They have disappeared.'

'Yes. They are very good at that. I think we will not find them by searching, as we do not know what to search for ... They must be lured to a place of our choosing, and there trapped.'

'Lured with what bait?'

'With the product of my factory. Yes. They must be allowed to see the product, thinking that we have tried to hide it but that they are cleverer than we are. They must be allowed to follow it, believing themselves unseen, in that truck, to somewhere convenient to ourselves— '

'And there killed. So be it.'

'No.'

'*No?*'

'Of course they will in due course be killed,' said Mustafa Algan patiently, 'but I am highly interested in them, and I want to talk to them first. Proper treatment of the girl will open very wide the mouth of the man. I take it that they were proposing to embark on operations competitive to my own. That has been my assumption since Şefik Bozkurt betrayed us to them, and it remains the only logical assumption. They have contacts, then, a market. It may be helpful for us to get those contacts, to secure that market. They may also have associates, who will wish to proceed with an operation competitive to ours. We should certainly know about those associates, so that we can kill them if they come here.'

'Very good, beyeffendi. Where shall we entice them?'

'To Ortahisar. To the place of seeds. It suits me to go there, in order to make dispositions with regard to that irritating Russian. I shall thus kill, as the English perplexingly say, two birds with one stone.'

Carpets were loaded onto the truck from the house which was larger than it looked. Several people watched, unsurprised, since carpets were woven in the house. They were rolled, wrapped in sacking, corded. There were not many – a dozen or fifteen. The truck was guarded.

The man in the grey Homburg and the clean-shaven man got into the cab of the truck. The man in dirty overalls was called from the back of the truck, where he was squatting among the carpets. He, too, climbed into the cab. The truck was laboriously turned in the narrow lane.

'Now,' whispered Colly.

Colly and Jenny, moving like the shadows of monkeys, were in the back of the truck among the carpets.

The truck went back to Konya, then turned east. It travelled all day and night.

176

Chapter 12

'Morphine,' said Colly, examining the white powder on his fingertip.

He wiped his hand thoroughly on a dirty rag of handkerchief. He had a horror of drugs. He did not want the minutest particle of this evil stuff to get inside him. None did.

The truck had started again after a brief stop in Niğde. It trundled now through immensely high, bleak, bare country, empty and hostile, lunar in its stony rejection of all life.

Very carefully they had untied a carpet, unrolled it, and found – nothing.

'Like that ghastly night near Bursa,' said Jenny. 'Hunt the thimble with no thimble.'

They tied up the carpet again so that it looked, they thought, exactly as it had looked. It was difficult and exhausting to manhandle the heavy roll of carpet in the back of the jolting truck, without making bumps which the men in the cab would hear. Their constant terror was that the driver would stop the truck while they had a carpet unrolled.

They looked at a second carpet, and a third.

'That night was bad enough when it happened,' said Jenny. 'Reliving it is more than I can bear.'

The fourth carpet they unrolled contained, in the middle, a fat cardboard tube. The tube was packed with white crystalline powder.

'I guess some more of the rugs have a supercargo

like this,' said Colly, 'but I'm not gonna look.'

'Well,' said Jenny, 'Sandro was dead right from the off. About Şefik too, I'm afraid. It all fits.'

'Some fits. Some not. I guess we travelled with raw opium from Finike to Antalya, and there was raw opium under all those other loads of fruit and stuff we saw going into the barn.'

'The crate they dropped was apples.'

'That's a little weird. Maybe it was one they kept for the cops to look at. Anyway, there obviously wasn't room in that shed to extract morphine from the raw stuff, so it was still raw opium in those machinery boxes. As far as Sille, a community I'm goddam glad to have quit. That house was where they produced this innocent-looking poison, with genuine carpet-making as a cover, as a reason for keeping the door locked. That all fits just fine. And it fits with Şefik's murder, that ambush we ran into, the bomb in the yacht. That's all normal stuff to guys in this trade, who are the most cynical, dangerous and anti-social criminals in the world. What doesn't fit is those poppies. Pink and red, for Christ's sake. What do we make of that?'

'I expect they painted them, like the roses in *Alice in Wonderland*.'

'Yeah. Another thing that doesn't fit is the way this truck is headed. Going north now, into the middle of Cappadocia, the back of beyond. They have a load of this stuff hidden in these drapes, worth God knows how many million bucks, why not take it to Istanbul or Smyrna?'

'Another odd thing is, why are they breaking with precedent?'

'Hey?'

'No sentry in the back here. It's almost as though they *wanted* us to creep aboard and find the stuff.'

'Could that be? No, baby, it's impossible. Think. They must assume we'd jump out and holler for the watch. The cops would find this stuff in a minute, an enormous haul. The Turks are terrifically down on dope of all kinds, except to sell to foreigners, and our chums up front would go to chokey for a long, long time ... Unless they think we're crooks too? In cahoots with little Şefik, who was maybe double-crossing them? Is that possible?'

'Even if it is,' said Jenny, 'and even if this is a trap, and even if they've spotted us, we've got to keep quiet and go along with it.'

'On account of our fat Italian friend. I guess he is a factor.'

'Also, there's one's own tiny niggle of curiosity.'

'Like about pink poppies. There sure is. Another factor. Right. We'll play along with it. I'll keep a little of this talcum, as another exhibit for later. A few grains, a lot of doses. I hope nobody catches me with this. Our chums won't miss it, and if they do they'll just have to be brave.'

The twin-engine Beechcraft flew the four hundred miles from Istanbul to Kayseri in time for lunch. Its elderly passenger was helped – quite unnecessarily – from the aircraft to a jeep. He set off with three companions westwards, towards Ürgüp and Ortahisar.

'Though in many ways I am old-fashioned,' sighed Mustafa Algan, 'in my respect, for example, for the traditional decencies of behaviour, I do find these aeroplanes convenient. Distressingly expensive, but sometimes actually worth the exorbitant cost. We shall be able to greet our visitors on their arrival, instead of requiring them to be held until our arrival. They might *not* be held. Süleyman and his colleagues have not greatly impressed me these last few days, whereas that man and that young woman *have* impressed me. It is thoroughly desirable that I should be there when they come to Ortahisar. Besides, it is more polite.'

The truck skirted the western face of the Melendiz

179

mountains. The road passed only a few miles from a towering, snow-capped mountain, an obviously extinct volcano, which dominated like an unfriendly god the dreary Cappadocian plateau. They turned east again, and came down into the drab little town of Nevşehir. Beyond it, the bleak country became bleaker still. There had been fat vegetables in the market at Nevşehir – Jenny gazed at them hungrily from the back of the truck – but it was impossible to guess how or where they were grown in this dead landscape.

They went through a weird, hardly credible valley of soaring rock pinnacles of different colours, utterly barren, beautiful, frightening. The white and rose and honey-coloured gorges between the pinnacles might have been the gates of heaven or of hell. Colly, dimly remembering a guide-book, said they were in the Valley of Fairy Chimneys.

'Chimneys?' said Jenny. 'There's no smoke without fairies.'

'Ha ha,' said Colly mirthlessly.

He was more and more puzzled by the direction in which they were travelling. He was more and more certain that Jenny was right – the hook had been baited, and they had taken the bait. Well, it was one way to discover something. They might be running their necks into nooses: but if they ran away from the ropes they would never know any more, and Sandro was a convicted murderer.

They came to a crossroads, where an incongruous modern motel and gas station faced an ancient building like a prison. They turned north. The road was bad. They bumped into another narrow valley. They left the road, and went very slowly along a re-entrant, a winding tributary valley. Everything was stone and scree, utterly barren and lifeless. The harsh sun blazed on bare grey rock. They were among more soaring pinnacles, of strange contorted shapes, into which it seemed that doors and arches had been cut.

'My God,' said Colly. 'These are the churches. The underground monasteries.'

'There's no such thing.'

'There is, too. The monks hacked these places right out of the rocks. Gave them somewhere to hide from Romans and Ottomans and such.'

'That's a church? That thing like a granite loofah the mice have been at?'

'Sure is. Hollowed out inside. Cells, chapels, grave-yards, all the fixings.'

The truck stopped. It could have gone no further on the rocky ground. All about were the weird shapes of the rock monasteries, monoliths gouged with doors and windows and flights of steps.

'We'd better get out of here,' whispered Jenny.

'Once we do, hiding is no problem.'

They heard the doors of the truck open. The men in the cab jumped down. There were murmuring voices, the voices of the three men. There was no sound of other voices, or of the movement of other people. Footsteps crunched away over the stony ground.

A complete silence fell.

'Let's take a peek,' said Colly softly.

With the utmost caution he leaned out of the back of the truck, and surveyed as much of the surroundings as he could see. The community of monoliths was startling, deeply impressive, but this was no time for sightseeing. The three men had squatted in the shade of a rock, fifty yards from the truck – the man in the grey Homburg, the clean shaven man, and the man in dirty overalls. They were smoking. They were, Colly thought, waiting for someone. They had not left a guard on the truck because there was nobody here, could be nobody in this lifeless wilderness.

They were waiting for someone with another vehicle, who would take the carpets and their contents, the enormous cargo of illicit morphine which would be smuggled out of Turkey into Europe, and probably

181

turned into heroin and peddled on the streets of cities.

'But why here?' murmured Colly. 'This is a ridiculous place to bring carpets, and it's a ridiculous place to bring morphine— '

'But,' said a voice close beside the truck, 'it is a sensible place to bring you.'

The voice was light, precise, a gentle high tenor. The English it spoke was almost perfect, almost unaccented.

Round the corner of the truck, into Colly's view, strolled a small elderly man. He stepped delicately, on neat little feet. He was intensely elegant: he wore a white suit of unmistakable Savile Row cut, with a pink silk shirt and foulard tie of subdued pattern. His face was aquiline, his eye sharp, his nose high-bridged; his copious silver hair, beautifully brushed, rose from his neat little head like the crest of a bird.

They had been frisked but not thoroughly searched. Nothing was found on Jenny. Colly's gun and knife were found and taken. The few dead poppies and the little packet of morphine, hidden in the seat of his trousers, were not found.

A second, smaller truck had appeared, followed by a jeep. The carpets had been transferred into the smaller truck, which had been driven away at once. Into the bigger truck had been loaded plastic sacks labelled as chemical fertilizer. The bigger truck had bumped away towards the main road.

'Seed,' said Mustafa Algan chattily. 'It comes to us here from the east. This is a convenient staging-post, and the rock churches are *very* convenient granaries. The seed is going down the coast, you know, to my friends the farmers. They are poor people down there, as I expect you saw, and delighted to add another valuable crop to their apples and oranges and wheat. Such a pretty crop, too. You could not forbear to pick some of my flowers, Lady Jennifer, could you? Progress is in some ways a great blessing. A poppy with all the virtues of the best

182

conventional poppies – indeed, more virtues than even the best of our old poppies – which has, as it were, inbuilt camouflage. Modern technology is full of wonders, and I speak as a *very* committed traditionalist. For example, when they told me that you, a young English lady of respectable family, had *shot* one of my men with a gun, I was quite dumbfounded. Even though I know many parts of Europe quite well. Dumbfounded! I think I am using that word with accuracy? I do not believe, as a matter of minor but indubitable interest, that I have ever used that word before. "Dumbfounded." A nice word, most powerful and evocative. *Epaté*. But "dumbfounded" is better. English is a much richer language than French, or the Italian of your unfortunate friend. I speak as one who knows all these tongues pretty well perfectly, if I may say so without offensive conceit, as well as a number of others ... Well well, we must not stand here chatting in the sun. Will you come with me, please? I beg you not to abuse my hospitality in any way, Mr Tucker. Each defiant or unfriendly gesture from you will cause Yildirim to cut off one of Lady Jennifer's fingers. Yildirim will *not at all* enjoy doing that, but he is very obliging to me, since he regards me as an old friend and benefactor.'

Yildirim was a scrawny, balding man, neatly but shabbily dressed in a dark suit and cloth cap. He had the usual ferocious Turkish moustache. If he was reluctant to cut off Jenny's fingers, he showed no signs of it. He carried a pair of heavy wire-cutters from a tool-box in the back of the jeep. It was sickeningly easy to picture the wire-cutters closing on a finger.

They walked towards the nearest rock church, Mustafa Algan stepping over the rough ground like the elegant bird he resembled. Colly followed him with a gun in his back. Jenny followed the gunman, Yildirim close behind her with the wire-cutters. A second gunman brought up the rear.

'Some of the churches like these,' said Mustafa Algan

affably, 'have become considerable tourist attractions. Of course, those are the major monasteries, the ones with big paintings and the like. You will find St George slaying his dragon. He was Cappadocian, you know. I wonder why your country adopted him, Lady Jennifer, or he your country? Curiously enough, you will also see St Theodore and St Demetrius and St Prokopion slaying dragons. I am prepared to wager that neither of you, though Christians, have ever even heard of St Prokopion. Here we go. Lower your heads for the arch. I am not obliged to do so, as you see. Smallness of stature has its advantages. Of course, some small men have, ah, overcompensated. I believe that is the psychologists' jargon. They have become tiresomely aggressive and acquisitive. I can imagine some naïve psychologist instancing me as an example of this phenomenon. But I seriously doubt if that is so. I am simply greedy. I love making money. Doctor Johnson, you know, the great lexicographer, once said that making money was the most innocent of all human activities. I do not *quite* agree with him, but I find the remark comforting, from such a source ... Here we are. There is supposed to be a connection between this place and St Enoyfrios, another worthy of whom I bet you have not heard....'

They were in a long chamber carved out of the living rock, approached by a narrow tunnel in which Colly had had to stoop, then opening out into a considerable vault. One of the gunmen put a powerful electric lantern on the floor. It illuminated paint-daubed walls, some niches, some evident graves, and a stone altar.

'Our seed store,' said Mustafa Algan. 'Now alas empty, but shortly to be refilled, I trust. That is one reason for my coming to Cappadocia. You are the other reason. Will you please, Mr Tucker, start telling me all the things that you must know I want to know. Please start immediately, and be extremely frank. Both delay and disingenuousness will, like more overtly physical irritations, occasion the removal, near the base, of as

184

many of Lady Jennifer's fingers as I consider suitable. When she has no fingers left, Yildirim will cut off other things. We can safely leave the choice to his ingenuity. I may say that I can listen, and you can talk, quite as well however many parts of herself Lady Jennifer loses. Her condition is therefore entirely up to you.'

Mustafa Algan, birdlike as ever, walked delicately to the stone altar and sat himself on it. Perched, with his legs swinging, he looked like an intelligent elderly schoolboy.

One of his men gestured to Colly, with the muzzle of his gun, to squat on the floor of the cave. Jenny was made to stand beside an iron spike which had been driven into the stone wall of the cave. One of her wrists was tied to the spike with thin cord. Yildirim stood beside her, the wire-cutters a few inches from her imprisoned hand. Colly was still not tied up. He was just as helpless as if he had been.

In the light of the lantern on the floor, Jenny's hand cast a shadow on the ochre-daubed wall of the cave. The shadow looked like an animal: like the animal-shadows which uncles make on the walls of nurseries to amuse young children. The wire-cutters cast a shadow nearby. The shadow of the wire-cutters looked like wire-cutters.

'Well, Mr Tucker? You have the floor. That is not an intentional joke, although, as a matter of fact, I think it is rather a good one. There is never a moment when inoffensive drollery is inappropriate. I hope you agree? But I do not want a stream of jests from you. You know what I want. Tell me.'

Colly felt utter despair. They had, before, been in places from which there seemed small chance of escape. They had never before been in a place from which there was no chance of escape. Mustafa Algan would not be satisfied with the truth. Even if he were, he would not let them go. He had declared himself to them, blithely, unworried. That meant that he had decided on their deaths. There was no doubt about that. The choice was

185

whether Jenny would die mutilated or unmutilated. It would make little difference to her in the long run, but the mutilation would be unendurable agony in the short run. Mutilated or not, Jenny would surely be raped before she was killed, probably by Yildirim and both the other hoodlums. There was nothing she or Colly could do about that.

Sandro was a dead man, too.

Colly could make time by talking. Time for what? At least he could, perhaps, save Jenny's fingers and other parts of her by talking.

Save them for what?

Suddenly Jenny began to talk.

She said, 'I can explain better than Colly can. I can't explain very well if you start cutting my fingers off, but I can explain *very* well if you'll kindly leave my fingers on. Well now, I don't know how much you know about the British aristocracy, Algan Bey, but what you must understand is that life has got very tricky for them, poor darlings. There's surtax and capital gains tax and capital transfer tax and inflation and dreadfully bumptious servants, always wanting bigger wages and shorter hours, and one thing and another, and people like us are not nearly as comfy as we used to be. So, my Papa, who used to be *very* comfy, decided he needed an entirely new source of income which wouldn't be spotted by the tax people. D'you follow me so far? So, one day about a year ago, my Papa called me into his study, and he said— '

At this point, as though quoting her father, Jenny suddenly let out an earsplitting, agonised, totally unexpected scream.

Every eye swivelled inevitably to Jenny. There was an astonished split second in which nobody was looking at Colly. Colly bounced up off the ground and butted the nearer gunman in the midriff with his head, knocking him into the other gunman. A gun went off beside his ear. He bore one guard to the ground. At the same time he flailed out with his feet, trying to kick the electric lantern on the floor. There was another explosion. He felt a savage pain in his right thigh. It was a wound which would pretty well disable him. He missed the lantern with his foot. With the tail of his eye he saw that Jenny had karate-chopped the man with the wire-cutters, with her free hand. She was desperately trying to untie the knot holding her other wrist.

Struggling with the guards on the floor, one half underneath the other, Colly felt an explosion in the back of his head. Darkness engulfed him.

He came to only a few seconds later, he thought.

Both gunmen were on their feet and holding their guns. Yildirim, the man with the wire-cutters, was on his knees sobbing and clutching his throat. Jenny had failed to undo the cord which bound her left wrist to the iron spike.

Mustafa Algan was moaning and clutching his knee.

He spoke slowly, with difficulty, through clenched teeth, so that although he spoke Turkish Colly found it easy to understand him. He said, 'You fool. You have shot me. In the knee. I can hardly bear the pain. You must take me at once to the doctor in Ürgüp. In the jeep. But I do not think I can stand the pain ... Wait. Before you carry me to the jeep. That pig on the floor was in my truck. With the rugs, with the morphine. He found the morphine. I heard him say so. He stole some. He must have. Search him. Give me half a grain of morphine. A little more than that. Search him! This pain is past bearing. I am too old to be shot. I am too rich.'

Already the guards were roughly searching Colly, pulling the clothes off him. He screamed from the pain of the bullet wound in his thigh. He was slapped when he screamed. They found the morphine in its filthy twist of handkerchief, with the bunch of wilted poppies.

'Quickly, quickly,' grunted Mustafa Algan. 'Bring it to me. I can measure the amount I need. Allah be thanked that I can take it by the mouth. Ah, let it work quickly, let it work quickly! This pain is too much for an old man ...'

One of the guards hurried across the vaulted cave to his master, carrying the morphine in the handkerchief. He took also the electric lantern with him, so that Mustafa Algan could see to measure out his dose.

The other guard said, in Turkish, that hc would shoot Colly in the other leg or in the belly if he moved.

Yildirim was still on his knees, not far from Jenny. The wire-cutters were near her on the floor. Jenny was still tied to the spike,. But she was furtively working at the knot. It was easier for her to do so when the lantern was taken to the altar

Mustafa Algan took the morphine. He sat, with trembling hands, waiting for the pain-killer to take effect. His face, lit from below by the electric lantern on the floor, looked no longer like a bird but like some ghastly idol, with shadows cast weirdly upwards from his nose and chin.

And then the face was contorted into a still more ghastly mask. The mouth opened, and stretched into a horrible mad grin. He began to scream like a young cormorant. His limbs twitched and thrashed. He fell forwards off the stone altar, twisted towards it, jerking, as though tugged by wires, and began to smash his face onto the stone.

Jenny screamed. Colly cried out. It was impossible not to, at the sight of a body and a soul in unutterable torment.

The man with Mustafa Algan tried to restrain him, to pull him clear of the altar on which he was smashing his face and skull. Mustafa Algan could no longer scream but, gurgling wetly, he pulled away from the man who was trying to help him and again pounded his smashed face onto the stone.

The two guards were thunderstruck, appalled. They jabbered to each other, terrified, helpless.

'I'm free,' said Jenny suddenly.

Colly gritted his teeth, and hurled himself at the legs of the man who was covering him. The man's attention was on the horrible scene being played at the other end of the cavern. He went down hard, dropping his gun. Colly dragged himself to the gun and knocked the man out with it.

Jenny gave Yildirim another chop with the heel of her hand on the side of his neck. He went down. She picked up the wire-cutters. She stepped quickly up behind the man who was trying to help Mustafa Algan, and hit him on the back of the head with the heavy wire-cutters. She knocked him out.

Mustafa Algan was dead

'We'll tie these guys up,' said Colly between his teeth. 'Then let's get to that jeep. You still have your fingers, so give me a hand, will you, baby?'

'Yes,' said Jenny, who looked uncharacteristically near to tears. 'Cops or doctor first?'

'Cops. Did you get the number of the truck that went off with the carpets?'

'Yes, of course.'

'And our truck? The seed truck?'

'Yes.'

When the police were persuaded to move, they moved with impressive speed.

The small truck was stopped and searched in Kirşehir, half way to Ankara. The morphine was found and taken to Ankara for analysis. Colly's account of its apparent effects was confirmed by immediate experiments with some unfortunate laboratory animals.

The larger truck was stopped on its way into Konya. The contents of the fertilizer sacks were identified as poppy seed.

The house in Sille was entered and searched. Heroin, morphine and raw opium were found in the rooms beyond the room with the carpet loom.

Poppies were picked from the hills above Finike. To

the utter amazement of the government scientists in Ankara, it was confirmed that, colour notwithstanding, they were opium poppies.

Colly and Jenny were flown to Smyrna. There they picked out, after four identification parades, the man they knew who looked like a wrestler. A medical dressing was found on the man's shoulder, although his wound was healing well.

The man was not known to the police in Smyrna, but he was identified as a convicted criminal, who had served two short prison sentences, from Istanbul. He produced, with a convincing show of outrage, an alibi for the night of Şefik Bozkurt's murder. His alibi was a fat young whore from an inland village. It was a good alibi but not good enough. The girl was frightened of the police. She admitted at last that she had been paid the price of a dozen nights of love for one loveless night which began at one o'clock in the morning. It was the cracking of the phoney alibi, rather than the identification parade, which transferred suspicion from Sandro to the man who looked like a wrestler, and enabled Sandro's lawyers to get him out of the prison.

Nothing incriminating was found in the carpet shop of Mustafa Algan in the Great Bazaar of Istanbul. None of his staff was found, either. The Turkish government began the wearisome process of investigating the funds in the numbered account in the Zurich bank.

Colly's wound was painful, but the bullet had not touched bone or a major blood vessel.

Since none of Mustafa Algan's records were found, nor any of his staff, it was impossible to pinpoint his customers. It was impossible to say how much more bad morphine or heroin had already been exported to Europe, how much was hidden in Smyrna or other places.

All the remaining poppies that could be found were destroyed. Some raw opium was found in the barn at the edge of Elmali, and some in the storehouse in Antalya.

Both lots were destroyed. The morphine seized in Kirşehir was destroyed, and the seeds which were found on the way to Konya.

It was hoped that not much of Mustafa Algan's produce was in the pipeline to the streets of Europe. Nothing could be done about what there was.

'Our advice,' said Sandro's Turkish lawyers, 'remains correct in the light of the facts as they existed at the time that we gave it. Subsequent events have altered circumstances, but *when* we advised you, we were advising you correctly. Our bills have been sent to your hotel. They will be waiting for you when you return there. It would oblige us if you would kindly settle them before leaving Izmir.'

'My bill,' said Sandro's Italian lawyer, 'is here in my hand. It will save time if I give it to you now. You cannot say that I gave you wrong advice, because I gave you no advice at all.'

'Well, fatty,' said Jenny to Sandro on the slow boat north from Smyrna, 'it was interesting in parts. I did learn something. Stretch pants make a good catapult, that's what I learned. I call that a useful lesson. So our time wasn't entirely wasted.'

'No, *tesoro*,' said Sandro. 'Not entirely.'

In the Georgian Institute of Agricultural Science in Tbilisi, Krikor Grotrian sat in his laboratory feeling old and frightened.

He had delivered the last of his available seed to Ara Mandikian, in the hills above the village beyond Yerevan. He had said there was no more – could be no more. It was difficult and dangerous to produce more plants, for more seed. *Papaver somniferum grotriani* still did not breed true, since his project had been peremptorily halted by Moscow. He said all this to Ara Mandikian, who replied with threats. More threats had come since,

God knew whence. Somebody immensely powerful would take drastic action against Krikor Grotrian, unless seed was produced quickly and in quantity. Exposure to the Russian authorities, to his own cold-eyed Director, was the least of the disasters Krikor would suffer.

Yet to produce the seed was to invite suspicion. Discovery was inevitable, sooner rather than later. Krikor was very lucky not to have been caught already. If the authorities had been more imaginative, more scientific, they must infallibly have caught him already.

Krikor would probably go, after his inevitable exposure, to one of the mental hospitals people whispered about.

He was caught between two evils – two fates which, if not worse than death, were certainly no better.

He was a scrawny, aging man. He was a physical coward, and he knew it. His volatile, over-sensitive personality was crucified by what he faced. He could see no way out. There was none.

No way out, but a source of comfort meanwhile. Was he not, now, just such a tortured soul as he had laboured to find comfort for? Was not the relief of such suffering, mental as much as physical, what he had devoted the best years of his life to? Was he not entitled to a few grains of the fruits of all his labours?

From a clump of hidden plants of *Papaver somniferum grotriani*, Krikor Grotrian extracted latex, which he dried. From the latex he extracted its rich proportion of morphine.

He did not approve of drugs. He had not expected to have recourse to them. But he had not expected terror and despair.

He decided to experiment with half a grain, and to take it by injection.

Drummond, S.

A stench of
poppies